Advance Praise for *Surviving Dresden*

"There's no better experience than curling up with a good book that you can't put down. *Surviving Dresden* has it all: vivid characters and crisp prose all wrapped in a thriller. The authors blend their superb command of history with a novelist's pen to create a gripping novel."
—Patrick K. O'Donnell, bestselling author of *The Indispensables* and *Dog Company: The Boys of Pointe du Hoc*

"If you love history and suspense, you'll love *Surviving Dresden*."
—Nathaniel Philbrick, author of *In the Heart of the Sea* and *Valiant Ambition*

"An evocative, inventive tale of war and moral judgment. *Surviving Dresden* vividly brings to life one of the most controversial episodes of the Second World War."
—Rick Atkinson, Pulitzer Prize winning author of the World War II Liberation Trilogy

"An incredibly suspenseful, powerful story with a redemptive ending. Deserves a wide reading audience, even serious consideration for the big screen. Happy to offer my highest recommendation."
—Frank Price, Former Chairman and CEO, Columbia Pictures, and Former President, Universal Pictures

"*Surviving Dresden* is a beautifully crafted, historically rich work of fiction that views the approaching Dresden calamity, day-by-day, through the eyes of a riveting cast of characters…. A wonderful read about a truly haunting human story."
—David M. Oshinsky, Pulitzer Prize Winning Author of *Polio: An American Story*

"In a gripping and compelling story, Martin and Burris have made us see the firebombing of Dresden, feel the fright of Gisela as escape eludes her, grieve with Wallace as he struggles over killing civilians, and marvel at Albert as he risks all time and again. A tale—and a history—of heroism, endurance, and courage, not to be missed."

—**Alice Joyner Irby, author of**
South Toward Home: Tales of an Unlikely Journey

"*Surviving Dresden* offers a moving and insightful story of one of the great human tragedies in human history, told from the point of view of those who lived through it. A compelling read."

—**Edward G. Lengel, Chief Historian at the National Medal of Honor Museum**

"I cannot recommend too highly this compelling story, wonderfully told, about the perilous risks of life and death in Dresden during World War II. Truly an eye-opening, riveting historical novel."

—**David M. Rubenstein, Co-Chairman, The Carlyle Group**

"Step aside, Billy Pilgrim. *Surviving Dresden* exceeds Kurt Vonnegut's *Slaughterhouse-Five* in capturing war and its aftermath with depth and nuance."

—**Robert McDonald, Professor of History, United States Military Academy, West Point**

"Martin and Burris have produced one of the best historically-based World War II novels in a generation—or more. Fast-paced, *Surviving Dresden* is a must-read about how this horrible conflict adversely affected so many lives during the search for peace and an end to the killing in war-torn Europe."

—**Charles Neimeyer, Professor, Naval War College, Fleet Support Program/ Director, Marine Corps History (ret.)**

"A gripping tale of love and despair told with historical accuracy always in mind. This is a must-read for all those who enjoy a great story and want to see the history of World War II from a new perspective. This is historical fiction at its finest!"

—**Seanegan Sculley, author of *Contest for Liberty***

"'Thrilling' is the right word to describe this compelling, action-packed, character-driven, historical novel. The war scenes are particularly vivid, mixed poignantly together with a fascinating cast, including lead protagonists Gisela Kauffmann and Wallace Campbell. The amount of research factored into this novel is quite impressive. *Surviving Dresden* is destined to be a classic work of historical fiction."

—**Rachel Hoge, editor and author**

"*Surviving Dresden* beautifully captures the role of air power in seeking to bring an end to World War II in Europe, a conflict that once under way, struggled to stop the massive destruction of peoples and places amid amazing stories of unexpected human survival. A gripping read from beginning to end."

—**Randy Roberts, Distinguished Professor, Purdue University, and author of *A Team for America: The Army-Navy Game That Rallied a Nation***

SURVIVING DRESDEN

A Novel about Life, Death,
and Redemption in World War II

JAMES KIRBY MARTIN AND ROBERT BURRIS

PERMUTED
PRESS

A PERMUTED PRESS BOOK
ISBN: 978-1-64293-861-6
ISBN (eBook): 978-1-64293-862-3

Surviving Dresden:
A Novel about Life, Death, and Redemption in World War II
© 2021 by James Kirby Martin and Robert Burris
All Rights Reserved

Cover art by Cody Corcoran

PERMUTED
PRESS

Permuted Press, LLC
New York • Nashville
permutedpress.com

Published in the United States of America
1 2 3 4 5 6 7 8 9 10

*Dedicated to All Those Who Gave Their All Fighting
to Preserve Human Freedom in World War II*

"The Nazis entered this war under the rather childish delusion that they were going to bomb everyone else, and nobody was going to bomb them…. They sowed the wind, and now they are going to reap the whirlwind."
—Air Marshal Sir Arthur Harris
Head of Bomber Command
Royal Air Force, 1942

"For us, the night had lasted for twelve years…I thought this is Dante's inferno on Earth. And yet I knew that only in the midst of this inferno could we save ourselves. While the entire city was in mourning, we were rejoicing."
—Henny Brenner
The Song is Over

"War is hell. Total War is worse than hell. The only hope for civilization is to find the means to stop the killing, which when started takes on a life of its own."
—*Anonymous*

"Lips gasp for air…. The only sound is the rustling of golden leaves, the rustling flow of time: which was–is–will be…."
—Lithuanian poet Janina Degutytė, upon visiting Auschwitz twenty years after it was liberated

PROLOGUE
Munich, Germany
September 19, 1931

HER NAME WAS GELI RAUBAL. She was twenty-three years old. The time was close to 10 a.m. Knocking loudly on her locked bedroom door, two housemaids received no response. With one of their husbands helping them, they broke the door lock, rushed into her beautifully decorated room, and found what they feared the most. Geli was dead—her body sprawled on the floor, her nose broken, her face bruised, blood pooled around her midsection. On a sofa next to her putrefying body lay a Walther 6.35 pistol with one round fired. The weapon belonged to Geli's half-uncle, Adolf Hitler, age forty-two.

Soon the *Stadtpolizei* and a doctor arrived at the death scene. The doctor examined Geli's slender body. He estimated that she had been dead for several hours; possibly as many as twenty four. The bullet had torn into her body above her heart and traveled downward toward her left hip.

The local police and the doctor were joined by a group of officers from the newly formed Nazi party *Sicherheitsdienst des Reichsführer— the SS*. Behind them came another uniformed man, an officer of unde-termined rank who commanded the respect of the other Nazis present. He was of average height and had a scowled baby face. As the SS men meandered about the apartment, the local police stood back—gave them the space they so nonchalantly demanded. The doctor continued his work as the SS men intermittently conferred with their officer.

The ranking SS officer smiled, then introducing himself to the doctor: "My name is Rudolf Hess, a close associate and friend of Herr Hitler."

The doctor acknowledged Hess, then replied with his assessment: "She may have struggled to stay alive for a few minutes or even an hour or two. *Rigor mortis* indicates that she's been dead for several hours, maybe even a day. Let me add that she slowly drowned in her own blood that filled her lungs until she could not breathe. From the angle of the gunshot, the pistol was fired down through her chest, and from the bruises on her face and the trauma of her nasal fracture, it seems clear there must have been a horrific struggle."

Hess nodded and politely responded, explaining to the doctor that he was mistaken. At the most, Geli could only have been dead for two or three hours. The evidence was clear, and he was not to dispute the findings of the "investigation." The cause of Geli's death was suicide.

"Write your report that way, sir. Case closed," Hess stated, trying not to look too menacing. Ready to leave the room, Hess looked back at the doctor and mumbled, "I'm glad we understand each other."

The story was soon all over the local newspapers. Geli was in a stressed condition, distraught about her singing lessons and an upcoming public concert. Overly anxious, she committed suicide. There was no mention that Geli's room was directly connected to Uncle Alf's bedroom. And there was no mention that the killing weapon was his.

Hitler, through his public rants and hyperventilating speeches, had become the best known of the dissident politicians vying for political power in the debt-ridden German nation. Over and over, he told the German people that their fractured economy and personal financial woes were the result of crushing reparation payments that the June 1919 Versailles peace settlement, officially ending World War I, had placed on them.

Hitler repeatedly propounded the two enemies of all true Aryan Germans—scheming, money-grubbing Jews and Russian communists, such as the likes of partially-Jewish Vladimir Lenin. Intolerance and bigotry directed toward these people and the constant refrain of defining an identifiable "other" on which to focus hatred and bring about political unity had long since served to rally pure-blooded Germans to support Hitler's National Socialist German Workers' Party.

Geli had lived for more than two years in Hitler's lavish, nine-room Munich apartment on fashionable Prinzregentenplatz. Her mother Angela was Uncle Alf's older half-sister. She had started working for Hitler as a housekeeper a few years before he moved into his Munich apartment. During those years, teenager Geli had developed an affectionate relationship with her half-uncle. Hitler liked having her light-hearted disposition around him.

When Geli reached her early twenties, their relationship became oddly sexual. Uncle Alf enjoyed drawing nude pictures of Geli—his personal pornography.

By September 1931, Geli's budding desire to get away from Hitler was primary on her mind. She had become his virtual prisoner, and he was relentless in dominating every facet of her life. If she wanted to go out for an evening and have some fun when he was too busy with his politics, his selected Nazi underlings escorted her to social events. At the same time, Hitler, whose relations with women were invariably strange, was losing interest in Geli. He had begun to date blonde, blue-eyed Eva Braun, age nineteen in 1931, a flirtatious young woman whom Geli despised.

Everything came to a head late on the morning of September 18. Hitler had given Geli permission to get away and spend some time with her friends in Vienna. She was writing a letter to one of them when Hitler walked into her room.

"No, no," he said, "I've changed my mind. I'm not allowing you to go to Vienna."

Frustrated and disappointed, Geli raised her voice, "You promised! Why won't you let me live my own life, at least once in a while? I love you, but I desperately need some freedom. I feel like a slave!"

Hitler's eyes winced. His face began to tighten into an angry frown. He did not allow anyone to question his commands. He certainly would not stand to have this girl challenge his authority. In an instant, Hitler transformed from uncle to dictator. He shouted back: "I have it on good authority that you have told a few persons about our personal relations. I will not allow you to do that. I am the hope and the future of Germany and its people. I will not let you ruin my reputation!"

"That's disgusting. It is not true!" Geli fired back at him as she began to cry. "Please permit me to go. Let me have my own life, at least now and then."

Hitler composed himself, scoffed, and folded his arms in front of him. "I am told that you have been sleeping with a Jew, that you've talked about marrying him, and that you are pregnant by him. So, it is time to teach you a lesson."

Geli felt hysterical. She noticed the whip under Hitler's arm and that he was dressed in his uniform with his revolver. He now clasped his whip firmly in his hand.

"If I am pregnant, I know it is not your child," she said. "You may have tried to mount me, but you never had the staying power to get inside…. I am going to Vienna!"

Turning beet red, Hitler's arms lashed out. He struck her nose with his fist. He raised the whip and began to swipe at her face. Geli reached for his gun, but he snapped at her arm—forcing her to recoil.

With her nose bleeding, she leaped at him. Grabbing for the gun, she felt it in her hand. She wanted to shoot, even kill him. She tried to squeeze the trigger, but Hitler jerked the weapon upward, over her head. She tried to reach for his Luger as he held it over her, pointing down toward her chest. The gun erupted, and a bullet smashed into her body. He grabbed her, holding her body upright. He saw blood gushing from her chest. Geli's eyes froze. Pulling back in disgust, he let her near lifeless body fall forward onto the floor.

Fuming, Hitler placed his gun on a couch next to Geli and retreated back into his bedroom, adjacent to hers. He paced a few times in the room as he collected his wits. He picked up the phone to call his driver, Julius Schreck.

"Get my Mercedes over here. I need to leave for Nuremberg now."

"Yes sir. I can be there in forty-five minutes," Schreck replied.

"I said now, Schreck!" Hitler shouted into the phone. "Urgent Party business has come up. I will meet you out front in no less than thirty minutes!"

Hitler pawed over the clothes he was wearing. Not finding any blood stains, he quickly grabbed and jammed one of his ornate, quasi-military uniforms into a large carrying bag, then tossed in some socks, underwear, basic toiletries, and one of his whips.

Getting ready to leave, he hesitated, then walked slowly back into Geli's room. For a minute or so he stared at her body. She was still alive. He could see her still frozen, open eyes. He heard soft sucking sounds of her struggling for air.

"Goodbye my dear, precious Geli. I loved you, but only I can save Germany and build the Fatherland into the greatest of all nations. You were starting to get in the way. You betrayed me."

He turned, locked Geli's door from the inside that connected to his room, then strode into the living room toward the apartment exit. Just before he left, he passed by his elderly housekeeper, stone deaf Frau Dachs. Nodding to her and feigning a smile, he rushed out his front door and down one flight of stairs before walking briskly onto Prinzregentenplatz as Schreck pulled the Mercedes to the curb.

Once in the car, Hitler, Schreck later reported, seemed exceptionally agitated—at times he huffed, or jerked his head from side to side. The future Führer was mostly silent for the entire one hour drive to Nuremburg. From time to time, he would mumble to Schreck about the beauty of the countryside as they motored along the highway, but Schreck could not seem to engage him in any conversation. They pulled up in front of the elegant Hotel Deutscher Hof. Hitler sat in his room all afternoon. He had no visitors. That evening, he attended a lively dinner gathering of his loyal party members. They ate and drank well into the night. Boisterous songs were interspersed with political outbursts, endless anti-Semitic rages, anti-communist threats, and ridiculing of the spineless Weimar government. No one can say whether Hitler slept fitfully or calmly that night.

The next morning, he and Schreck climbed into the Mercedes. They would drive five hours north to Hamburg. Hitler was to be featured that evening in an extravagant Party rally, yet another opportunity to bluster about his core hatreds.

Close to noon, a speeding car caught up to them, motioning for them to pull over. The messenger was from the Deutscher Hof. Herr Hess had called about an emergency situation back in Munich. Something had happened to a young woman named Geli. That's all the messenger knew. He explained that Hitler should call back Hess as soon as possible.

"My god." Hitler feigned complete surprise and deep concern. "My god," he said to Schreck. "We must hope my beloved niece is not hurt. She is so dear to me," he said to Schreck in a soft tone, then ordered, "Find us the nearest phone."

Hitler smiled to himself as he climbed into the car that was now over 150 miles from the scene. He had his alibi. If she had died early that morning rather than yesterday, who could possibly implicate him in Geli's death? No one would dare to do so.

Geli was now forever gone. Any hint of scandal quickly faded away. Nosy reporters who expressed any lingering curiosity would have to answer to the Brownshirts of the SA—at best, they would be severely beaten. Hitler was personally responsible for the death of another person. Angela Maria "Geli" Raubal was among the first victims of her uncle's demand for complete obedience to his will. She would not be his last.

Less than a year and a half later, in January 1933, Adolf Hitler became the Chancellor of Germany. Now the seasons of stifling all political opposition took full bloom. Killing sprees eliminated competition in Hitler's accession to omnipotent dictator status.

Such was the "Night of the Long Knives" in 1934 from June 30 to July 2, Hitler's opponents—both real and suspected, many of them Nazi Party members—were hunted down and murdered. They included, of all people, the Führer's former close associate but now suspected chief rival, SA commander Ernst Röhm. When captured and imprisoned, he faced the unenviable choice of committing suicide or having two Nazi lackeys execute him. Röhm chose the latter option.

Even as the Führer purged all competition that might threaten his absolute power, he rattled on about the thousand-year reign of his envisioned Third Reich. His Aryan paradise was to be free of Jews, Gypsies, communists, homosexuals, handicapped persons, and other so-called societal and political deviants whom he and his racist, anti-Semitic inner circle of human killers felt compelled to first suppress and—ultimately—to exterminate. Should his adoring listeners miss the point, he told them in 1933 to boycott all business dealings with Jews. In 1935, the Nuremberg Laws ordered all pure-blooded Germans not to intermingle or engage in sexual activity with Jews. Hitler was sure their only goal, part of some fanciful international conspiracy, was to pollute the blood of superior Aryan peoples, since they were continuously plotting to take over the world.

The Führer dreamed of *"Lebensraum"*—gaining control of massive amounts of territory to the east and north of Germany for his future Aryan dreamland. First it was a small group of reactionary, bitter men. Then it became a party of enablers. A nation followed into a militaristic inhumane cult madness. What Hitler started morphed into World War II in September 1939 with his blitzkrieg invasion of Poland. His prison and death camps were already becoming operational before that moment when Luftwaffe bombers began the destruction of Poland's capital city, Warsaw.

By early 1945, millions upon millions of additional human beings had been maimed and killed, a ghastly price to pay for Hitler's lifelong quest to control everyone and everything around him. Unfortunately, all the killing would continue until the end of April 1945 when he finally did the world his greatest favor and committed suicide—ironic, indeed, as a way for Uncle Alf to end his destructive life, given what had happened to his presumably adored half-niece back in 1931.

PATHWAY NEWS SERVICE,
Update, February 1, 1945
Auschwitz-Birkenau

Soviet Offensive

On January 27, the 322nd Rifle Division of the USSR's Red Army marched into the small town of Oswiecim, Poland. Many of the soldiers rode astride mottled, tired ponies. They were part of the vital campaign to push back German offensive operations in eastern Europe. What they found was very disturbing.

Reports state that the Russians were weary and on edge of a possible Nazi ambush as they entered what turned out to be a large Nazi concentration camp just outside the town's center. There, the soldiers discovered the emaciated bodies and hollow eyes of vacant skeletal beings observing them from behind barbed wire. Behind them, hundreds of decaying corpses lay frozen on the ground.

The Soviets had stumbled upon what was left of the Auschwitz–Birkenau Nazi death camp. The death camp guards, according to prisoners who could still speak, were SS troops. They had fled, based on one estimate, with more *than 7,000 men, women, and children, all of them sick, starving, freezing, and many on the verge of death. No one yet knows how many of these unfortunate souls will survive in freezing winter weather as they are forced to march back toward Germany.*

Among the few left behind and still alive, they described barbaric treatment, chronic malnutrition, daily "selections" for showers, backbreaking work details, bizarre medical experiments, and recreational SS violence. One soul, still able to walk, led the soldiers to huge piles of discarded clothing—enough for a million people, he claimed. They also found several tons of human hair. Apparently, the showers—gas ovens, in actuality—had been used for the past three years.

Most of the victims were Jews, purposely exterminated as demanded by Adolf Hitler and his loyal Nazi followers, both military and civilian—what they called the "Final Solution."

Before liberating Auschwitz-Birkenau, Soviet forces had taken Warsaw, as well as Estonia, Latvia, Lithuania, and Belorussia. Experts now believe that many more such death camps will be found and liberated as Allied forces moving both east and west into Germany, begin the final struggle to crush the Nazi regime.

PATHWAY NEWS SERVICE,
Late Edition, February 1, 1945

Allied Victory in Belgium

Just like their Russian allies, British and American forces are now advancing toward Berlin. On January 29, two days after the liberation of Auschwitz, they finally turned the tide against a major German offensive into Belgium's Ardennes Forest. The bloody Battle of the Bulge, as it's now being called, lasted a month and cost the Allies thousands of lives.

With the Germans now reeling backward, morale has surged upward again among the allied troops. Major Frank Kissling, a spokesman for General George S. Patton, commander of the U. S. Third Army, said: "Thank God. We've broken them. They are in full retreat. Soon we'll be crossing the Rhine River. Then it's onto Berlin."

Queried further, Kissling stated that Patton had every intention to reach Berlin before the Red Army and finish off Hitler and his Nazi fanatics before the Soviets got there.

In related news, reports have been pouring into our press room that Hitler has ordered all Germans to fight to the death. All males between the ages of sixteen and sixty must enroll in the Volkssturm, or people's national militia, to join in this total war to rescue the faltering Third Reich.

In London, our reporter caught up with Home Secretary, the Right Honorable Herbert Morrison, usually a man of few words. Smiling about the major victory in Belgium, he said, with excitement: "We've got them on the run. My prayer is that the German people will rise, take down Hitler, and surrender before more needless killing. But I'm not optimistic that will happen."

ASKED WHY, MORRISON REPLIED: "LOOK up in the sky. Thousands of our civilians have been maimed and killed right here in England in recent months. The Nazis keep launching V-1 doodlebug and V-2 rockets against us. But they can't break our will. The question is whether we can break theirs before everything is destroyed over there—and thousands more lives are lost."

"That bad?" asked the reporter.

"Yes, indeed, I'm afraid so," replied Morrison. "Let me add, for the record: the blood on Hitler's filthy hands is a stain of unparalleled proportions on human civilization. We can't yet say for sure. The fighting's not over yet. But this devilish maniac may be responsible for thirty, forty, maybe even fifty million deaths, an unimaginable tragedy inflicted on the decent people of this world."

Our reporter then asked: "What's next? And what is Prime Minister Churchill thinking and doing? We haven't seen him around the past couple of days."

"Two good questions. We will conquer Hitler's regime. As already publicly stated, the Allies will accept nothing less than unconditional surrender. We will hit them with everything we have, both on land and from the air. Of course, I can't give you more details, but expect increased bombing runs to destroy their fuel supplies, their rocket launching pads, and their war-related industrial capacity. We are into total war and will not stop until Hitler blinks or passes from the scene. Our challenge is how to stop the killing when the enemy won't stop the killing." He paused, and then added, "Any final questions? I must get moving to an important war cabinet meeting."

The reporter repeated the earlier question about the Prime Minister.

"Oh, yes, sorry," said Morrison. "You know, Churchill is tireless, working morning, noon, and night. He's delighted about the news from Belgium, and he's sent his congratulations to Allied Commander-in-Chief Dwight Eisenhower and generals in the field. He now sees an end to this god-awful war, even if our Royal Air Force planes must keep bombing German industrial cities into oblivion. That's all I can tell you right now. Oh, yes, you will be hearing from him soon, but his current movements are top secret."

GISELA
February 3, 1945
Ten days before the Attack

THE FIRST MENTION OF DRESDEN, widely known as the "Florence of the Elbe," a place of beauty and splendor, appeared in the early thirteenth century. Over the centuries the city developed a reputation as one of the greatest seats of high culture in all of Europe. Dresden attracted artists, writers, and intellectuals from across the continent. In 1798, the poet Jean Paul wrote, "When you step onto the Dresden Bridge, palaces the size of towns lie before you, and beside you the river Elbe flows from one distant realm into another. You see faraway mountains, plains, solitary little ships, and on the bridge itself an ever-changing procession of people, a long avenue, and the bustle of life engulfs you."

By 1945, Jean Paul would not have seen a procession of artists, thinkers, and dreamers streaming across Dresden's bridges. Instead, a choking flood of refugees from the Eastern front kept moving through the city. They were escaping from their destroyed homes and broken lives, hoping for survival. Their one dream was that the war would end and they would still be alive to see a new day without unending killing.

As people stumbled along, families huddled close together, carrying all their remaining possessions on their backs and in carts. The war had beaten them down as they struggled to move forward with their strained, overburdened carts. They were survivors fleeing rapacious Russian forces, leaving them with memories of relatives now dead and their homes in rubble and dust.

The refugees tried to ignore the nervous whispers of a city on the edge, wondering about its fate as the war dragged on. They came to Dresden forlorn and hungry—for food, for shelter, for a reason to hope. And yet...despite the chaos, the crush of humanity, business still carried one way or another throughout most of the city. Men and women walked to work; old men sat in front of nearly barren sidewalk cafes to play checkers and chess.

The cold inside the massive, thrumming Goehle Zeiss-Ikon factory stabbed at Gisela Kauffman through her worn wool coat, making her bones throb and her knuckles ache. Dozens of women like her—yellow stars stitched onto their clothing—worked silently, hunched over conveyor belts bearing intricate metal components. They squinted in the ashen darkness, the few shreds of feeble, gray light piercing the dirty windows failing to illuminate weary, calloused hands as they worked.

In a place condemned to an endless cycle of drudgery and deprivation, Gisela tried to imagine the world that existed outside the factory walls—a world in which hope still somehow managed to survive. But it was useless. Any winter light remained outside. Within these somber, concrete walls, darkness ruled.

Despite Dresden's renown as one of Europe's great cultural centers, the city was home to a thriving industrial sector that helped drive the Nazi military machine. Manufacturing in the city was fueled by forced labor—Gisela and other Jews, half-Jews, and other prisoners—who pumped out weapons and equipment for Hitler's collapsing war effort, day after day after day. The Goehle Zeiss-Ikon factory produced military gun sights. Other factories had been converted to produce radar and electronics components, gas masks, aircraft engines, and parts for German U-boats.

At the Goehle Zeiss-Ikon facility, Gisela worked at a conveyor belt, a link in the assembly line that seemed never to end. Always, over their shoulders and in the shadows of grinding, deafening, mechanical presses and drills, Gisela knew she and the others were being watched by Nazi plant managers and guards. No one dared waver from their automaton behavior—even the slightest move askew would bring harsh consequences. The charge of inefficiency was severe, perhaps crippling. The accusation of sabotage was death.

Standing at an assigned position on the conveyor for hours on end, adding the same parts to an unending stream of metal, Gisela ignored the pains in her body. Repeating the same task, over and over again for hours, meant the aches in her back and knees were fierce—acting in concert with her disillusionment and sorrow about her life.

For the decade leading up to and during the war, Hitler's Nazi Germany built one of the most extensive forced labor systems in recorded history, putting over 20 million concentration camp prisoners, civilians, and POWs to work in fields, factories, and mines. Forced labor was central to the Führer's policy of exploiting and persecuting Jews, beginning in the mid-1930s, eventually to be followed by the "Final Solution" of mass killings.

During the 1930s, Hitler's anti-Semitic policies exacerbated the situation, limiting the ability of Jews to run their businesses or earn a marginal living, and ultimately, driving many Jews into destitution and poverty. Even those who desperately sought to escape from Germany often lacked the financial resources to do so. And many nations throughout the world had closed their doors to Jewish refugees.

By the middle of 1938, Hitler ordered that Jews could be deemed criminals without evidence and be put to work in excavation and mining efforts. Those who had been cast into poverty became easy targets. Crimes that resulted in sentencing to a forced labor camp included minor traffic infractions or alleged charges of disturbing the peace.

While authorities examined non-Jewish criminals and anti-Nazi citizens for their fitness for manual labor, no such standard existed for

Jews: they were simply rounded up and sent to the camps. However, when this general policy failed to reduce the number of Jews in Germany or supply the needed labor to support the ever-growing war effort, the Nazis began to employ harsher regulations that sentenced nearly 60,000 Jews to mandatory, uncompensated work assignments. They became Hitler's slaves before facing death in concentration camps, with Dachau, Buchenwald, Auschwitz-Birkenau among the worst.

In Dresden, Jews—and then half-Jews, like Gisela—were the slaves at the Goehle Zeiss-Ikon plant. They suffered from malnutrition, disease, fatigue, and physical abuse, not only from the guards at the factory, but also from hostile non-Jewish civilians they encountered walking to and from the plant every day.

The armed guards who kept close watch on Gisela and the others alternated between patrolling the factory and watching the workers from observation stations. From these vantage points they could quickly evaluate whether production goals were being met and identify those who needed swift discipline.

Gisela knew she was always being watched. The knowledge of this scrutiny was as oppressive as the mind-numbing, soul-deadening repetitive work. She was very aware of what happened to those who dared to fall out of line or faltered in their assignments from sickness or fatigue. She remembered her friend Henny, who one day began crying and shouting at no one and everyone, driven mad by the dullness, despair, and lack of hope in her life. One of the guards beat her with a whip. He could not get Henny under control, so he pulled out his Luger pistol and shot her dead on the spot.

Then there was Anja, gifted in chemistry. She hoped to become a doctor one day, but then collapsed at her post with what was a routine case of bronchitis. Two guards hauled her from the factory floor to the bleak courtyard at the rear of the facility, where the workers were allowed a ten-minute break every four hours. The sharp sound of a gunshot that reverberated over the incessant din of the factory's machines left no doubt as to her fate—or of anyone else who exhibited similar weaknesses.

Out of the corner of her eye, Gisela noted Albert Schmidt, wearing the uniform of the Wehrmacht Home Guard. Gisela was sure that Albert was unlike the other guards. She had known him from their school days. Now, barely twenty-one, he should have been at the front and, indeed, had served in Silesia only a few months earlier, until a bullet from a Soviet PPSh shattered his left forearm. The subsequent gangrenous infection necessitated his arm's removal from the shoulder down. It was a miracle that he had survived at all.

Gisela wondered whether he would have preferred to die a hero's death to living life so physically damaged. Despite his piercing blue eyes, sandy hair, and rugged good looks, she was sure the wound humiliated him—that he felt incomplete.

Walking to work one day, she had witnessed Albert's shame when a non-Jewish Dresden resident had fawned over him, really just viewing him with pity. She had seen him diminished when smiles from a local single girl their age had changed when her eyes noticed the empty shirtsleeve pinned to his shoulder.

Gisela felt that it was more than a missing arm that set Albert apart from other German soldiers. At heart he was not a Nazi. Like so many others, Albert was just a local boy drafted into the war that Hitler was waging.

Despite Albert's attempts to affect a stern, dispassionate countenance, a gentleness emanated from his natural calm. Even when he would look away from her, Gisela could remember, could sense his kindness. On the rare occasion when their gazes met, she saw that it wasn't just the shame from his missing arm that unnerved Albert. He felt exposed in her eyes, as if she could see through his disguise and recognize him for who and what he truly was—a non-believer in Nazism who was counting the moments until the war would come to an end. This pleased him, but at the same time filled him with dread that she would share with others the truth of what she saw.

Back in their school days, Albert reserved his most robust teasing for her. His overtures became more explicit as the years went by. Although Gisela liked Albert as a friend, that was as deeply as her emotions ran. Albert persisted in his awkward attempts to gain her favor, until, at the age of eighteen, when Gisela became engaged to Jacob Gottlieb. Albert backed away, although Gisela could not be sure that he had given up hope.

Despite his uniform, and her situation, Gisela still felt there might be some affection. Unlike most of the dark-haired, brown-eyed women laboring at the factory, Gisela was blonde, with blue eyes that her father's Germanic features mirrored. A bright, clever mind—along with a resilient and restless spirit—further enhanced her natural beauty. Even as a child Gisela was the student who dared to point out when the teacher had made an error or to stand up when she believed she or one of her friends was being treated unfairly by an adult. Her father used to call her *mein wilder Hengst*—my wild stallion. Gisela was, in appearance and in substance, everything the Führer dreamed of, but with one basic difference: she was not Aryan.

Nearly two years had passed since Gisela's engagement to Jacob. Before the war, Dresden's Jewish community totaled around 26,000, about 5 percent of the city's population in 1940. Thousands of them were stripped of their property and possessions and then shipped off to various concentration camps. By early 1945, the number of Jews, or half-Jews, still residing in Dresden was no more than 200. A few had found some means to escape. But for Jacob and Gisela, it was too late.

One night in early 1943, Waffen-SS troops had hauled Jacob out of his bed. Rumor had it that he ended up in the Buchenwald death camp about 130 miles west of Dresden. Few prisoners survived there, often beaten or starved to death before their brutalized, lifeless remains were hung on hooks awaiting cremation. No one could say for sure whether Jacob was still alive; but the odds were that he was no more than human ashes, a thought that frequently brought Gisela to private outbursts of anger and enraged tears.

Albert, back from deadly combat in Silesia in July 1944, had not yet been assigned to guard duty at the Goehle Zeiss-Ikon plant. Early one morning he struggled to dress himself by using just his right arm.

His mother usually helped him put on his socks. That day, Albert was determined to put them on himself. It took him almost ten minutes just to do this simple, everyday task. A small victory. He looked at his boots. He could get them on, but he still had not mastered how to tie them. Another defeat.

That week his assigned duty consisted of walking the streets, making sure that all was calm. By nightfall he felt a hot blister on his right foot. Further on, his left foot began to chafe. He found a bench on Pulsnitz Street. Relief…if only for a few minutes. The streetlights were on, but there was not a single person in sight. He contemplated returning home.

Albert struggled to take off his right boot to examine the damage. It was then, at that awkward moment, that Gisela appeared around the corner.

Despite her pallor and thinness—the way that long days of grueling labor had worn her down in combination with a near starvation diet—Albert recognized her immediately. Her natural beauty had not changed. He wanted to call out to her. He raised his only arm, but then…hesitated. They were no longer classmates. They were no longer friends. He was a soldier. She was a laborer. That was all.

Regardless of his feelings, Albert was in the uniform that symbolized Hitler's hatred and demented use of power against Jews. His uniform cast Gisela as a parasite on Aryans. In his hysteria, Hitler had shouted and written that Jews consciously planned to poison the blood of Aryans. Albert believed none of such bashing. But to Gisela, what might she think when she saw this uniform? Would she turn away? Or spit on him and curse him? He would most certainly understand either reaction.

Albert lowered his arm. His shoulders sank as he simply watched her pass. He said nothing as she walked by. Gisela had seen Albert. She recognized him. But she did not see her friend. Gisela only saw his Wehrmacht uniform.

Gisela pushed the memories away and focused on her mind-numbing work. She sensed movement beside her. She looked up to see Rachel. Rachel was thinner than most, with dark circles under her eyes, and was clutching her stomach. Letting the bomb fuses pass before her untouched, Rachel lifted a trembling, sallow hand to her forehead.

"Keep working," Gisela urgently whispered to her friend.

Rachel could barely muster the energy to speak. "It's been hours. I can't anymore. I can't."

Gisela's eyes furtively darted toward the sentries on the observation platforms. Talking was strictly forbidden.

Albert's attention was diverted. But Master Sergeant Heinrich Gruber's was not. Gruber was a Nazi zealot, an intimidating muscular man in his mid-forties, no hint of humanity in his hard eyes or jowly face. The son of a brick mason and a seamstress, Gruber had gone to work for his father full-time when he was just thirteen. He was never a particularly bright or enthusiastic student. He did not continue his education beyond the middle grades. Gruber served briefly as a private during World War I. He then came up hard and fast as a SA Brownshirt brawler in Hamburg. He never met Hitler, but he had the kind of stolid, intimidating Aryan look that the future Führer most admired.

In many ways a natural-born thug, Gruber absorbed the dynamism, nationalism, and charisma that Hitler projected. He became enamored of Nazi doctrine: the pomp, camaraderie, and bloated militarism. Since he had trouble deciphering some of the more unfamiliar words, a friend had read portions of *Mein Kampf* to him on their work breaks at construction sites. Hitler's venomous rhetoric about Jews resonated within Gruber and others as a rallying cry.

Gruber had grown up listening to his father's endless rants, fueled by beer and schnapps, against the Jewish bankers and landlords whom he believed were bleeding German workers dry. When the Great Depression struck in 1929, there was no call for masons. Gruber's father's work vanished. His father drank himself to death in a matter of months, and his mother turned to scrubbing floors in the homes of the wealthy just to provide enough bread and soup for them to survive. A number of the families that employed her were Jewish. His dead father, and now his mother's situation, infuriated Gruber. Hitler and the Nazis tapped into the anger and resentment that had fueled Gruber's bigotry for years.

Gruber had considered it one of the great moments in his life when he rushed forward to enlist as a Wehrmacht soldier. He eagerly marched into Poland and took part in the relentless siege that led to the fall of Warsaw in September 1939. He was part of the massive assault on the Soviet Union, dubbed Operation Barbarossa, for nothing more than three weeks when a bullet from a Russian sniper's rifle tore into his abdomen, nearly killing him. He survived, but his injuries were severe enough that he was deemed no longer fit for combat. He threw himself into his new duties as prison guard at the Treblinka concentration camp, gaining a reputation for the savage pleasure he took in brutalizing helpless prisoners unfortunate enough to draw his attention.

Further inspired by such anti-Semitic propaganda films as *Jud Süß* and *Ohm Krüger*, Gruber's hatred of Jews festered and metastasized— feelings he released by beating and killing prisoners he always seemed to catch in the act of "trying to escape."

Gruber greeted his transfer in late 1944 to head overseer of the Goehle Zeiss-Ikon factory as a career setback. He was nothing if not a good and dutiful Nazi. Gruber had fewer opportunities to exact his cruelty on the women who worked at the factory. They were worth more alive than dead—Gisela knew full well that he relished the opportunity to enforce his brand of discipline whenever he had the chance. In one case, Gruber had taken a young Slavic woman outside and raped her while she begged for mercy. After he was done, he stood over her and began to kick her, over and over again, until she began to cough blood.

Gruber seemed to just enjoy the site of her convulsions as she cried out in tears while she choked in pain. He thought she should consider herself lucky. If she had been a Jew, he would have simply blown her brains out.

Killing Jews was just fine. Gruber knew that if he was caught raping a Jewess by the Gestapo, it could cost him his life. Not because of his actions, but because he had mingled his superior Aryan bodily fluids with a tainted Jewish woman.

Gisela sighed, feeling a moment of relief that Gruber was looking the other way too. He did not notice Rachel…this time.

Under the mechanical din, Gisela looked at her work, and without moving her lips said to Rachel: "Keep going. You must. We are here together. One moment to the next. Don't think of anything else. They might kill you."

Rachel's head sank as she demurred. "I don't have your strength. I don't care anymore."

Rachel had also gone to school with Gisela and Albert. But she was always a sickly girl who was frequently too weak to join in their games. Gisela and Rachel had bonded over their love of reading, a shared journey that had begun with the adventures of the Apache *Winnetou*, matured through Hesse's *Siddhartha*, confronted the challenging surrealism of Franz Kafka, and examined the experiences of Irmgard Keun's character Sanna during the rise of the Nazis that so closely mirrored their own. Absorbing, learning, growing, Gisela and Rachel had spent countless hours reading side by side, each escaping into the world of ideas before them, close enough to feel as if they were sharing every word.

"You do have the strength," Gisela encouraged. "If you don't work…."

Resignation clouded Rachel's drawn face. "What? They will beat me? Kill me? Send me to the camps? Why not? Sometimes I pray for it."

Gisela kept focused on the moving belt as she continued to beg her friend. "If you must pray for anything, pray for strength."

Gisela did not see that Gruber's eyes were now intently locked on her and Rachel. He was transfixed on them from one of the doors leading into the facility. Gruber moved purposefully down the stairs. Albert sensed the danger as he followed Gruber by only a few steps. Gisela saw the movement and her blood ran cold. To be caught would be—

"You there! Get back to work!" She heard Albert call out. "Now!"

Gisela looked up at Albert, who was rushing past Gruber. Thinking fast, Gisela came up with the only thing she hoped would throw these men off. "Her time came early this month. She is losing blood and is about to collapse."

Albert was acutely aware that he too was being observed. As he moved quickly to get in front of Gruber, he slowed down to block him from passing on the narrow factory aisle. He feigned a meticulous evaluation of Gisela's work while rapidly sorting through his options. He took Rachel by the arm. "You, come with me."

Albert coldly nodded to Gruber as he and Rachel approached. "Malingerer!" Albert barked as he pushed Rachel past Gruber. "I will see to it that she's properly motivated."

Gruber eyed them suspiciously; but then, to him, everyone and everything was suspicious. He did not trust Albert. This was not the first time that Albert seemed to deflect Gruber in the performance of his desire to punish.

The hissing sound of a ruptured steam line across the factory floor intervened. Easily distracted, Gruber gave Albert a grudging nod. He hurried over to make sure that the machinery's malfunction did not hinder or delay production.

As Albert pushed open the heavy metal door that led outside the building, Gisela saw his gaze travel back to her. She flashed an unspoken look of gratitude, then returned to her work. With Rachel gone, Gisela now had to do the work of two. But at least Rachel was now with Albert, not Gruber. Refusing to give in to the fatigue and nearly overwhelming sense of futility, Gisela focused on the monotony of the conveyor and her task—piece by piece, by piece by piece....

Entering a courtyard with several wooden benches scattered underneath a pair of barren beech trees, Albert helped Rachel sit down. She squinted up at the sun, a faint gauzy white orb behind the dense clouds, and closed her eyes. She felt the vague caress of mild winter warmth on her face. Checking to see that no one was watching, Albert pulled the canteen from his belt and offered water to her. She drank.

"Thank you."

Albert did his best to maintain a stern countenance. "Maximum production requires full effort. A successful war effort depends on each of us."

Rachel passed the canteen back to Albert. She could still see the boy that she had known so long ago. "I know you are kind to me because of Gisela."

Albert offered no response. He tightened the cap on his canteen and tucked it back into his belt.

"No need to pretend with me. I know you have adored her ever since we were in school. We all knew—"

"Times have changed," Albert barked back at her. "It doesn't matter anymore."

Rachel doubted his denial. She had touched a nerve.

"Albert. You must think about what might happen when the war ends. Especially now with Jacob more than likely—"

Albert's face tightened, and Rachel leaned closer. "If you really still have affectionate feelings for her, you must help us. Just until the Russians…."

There was a lot of talk that the Russians were no more than sixty miles away, but Albert still expressed what he was told. He adamantly shook his head. "Our troops are pushing back the Ivans. The tide has begun to turn—"

"You don't believe that. The Soviets are killers. They will not stop. The Americans and British to the west—we both know they will overcome Hitler's defenses. Sooner rather than later, I can only pray. Help us survive until they do."

Rachel could tell that her words had hit their mark. A bracing gust of wind swirled brown leaves in a frantic dance.

Albert finally broke down. He looked at Rachel with the schoolboy eyes she once knew. "We are all prisoners in one way or another. You have five minutes. Any more time and you'll be punished. If it's by

Gruber, we both know what that means…he will beat you, possibly rape you. Even kill you."

"Beat me, maybe, but rape me? No. It is ironic that Hitler's 'final solution' protects me from disgusting Aryan beasts like that. You know that I'm a Jew!"

Albert felt intense embarrassment, even as Rachel implored him again. "We were once friends. Please help us escape from this misery."

Inside the factory, Gisela glanced toward the steel door through which Albert had led Rachel to the courtyard. She was thankful for Albert's kindness toward her close friend, but reminded herself that he was one of *them*. He could not be trusted.

She redoubled her work efforts, making sure that Rachel's absence didn't slow down the production of bomb fuses.

WALLACE
February 3, 1945
Ten days before the Attack

THE BRITISH AVRO LANCASTER BOMBER was among the most destructive weapons that the Allies had in their wartime arsenal. Heavily armored with eight 0.303-inch Browning Mark II machine guns, by 1945 this aircraft could deliver a 10-ton blockbuster Grand Slam bomb, the most powerful non-atomic explosive deployed in the war. Some 69 feet long with a large bomb bay and a wingspan reaching 102 feet, this heavy bomber could cruise up to 2,500 miles before refueling. Powered by 4 Rolls-Royce, Merlin V-12 engines, Lancasters delivered over one third of the 1.5 million tons of bombs dropped on Germany during World War II. Each of these bombers carried a crew of seven men.

Just six years earlier, Flight Captain Wallace Campbell could not have imagined the circumstances under which he would be piloting a Lancaster over the land of Goethe, Hermann Hesse, and Thomas Mann. At university, he'd written his senior thesis on Mann's classic novel, *The Magic Mountain*. He had eagerly dissected the way the book explored the dynamic relationship between the spirit and the real world, and how compassion would bridge this seeming divide. Inspired by Mann and the praises of his professors, Wallace had briefly tried his hand at penning his own novel. He abandoned the effort when life got in the way.

Wallace was the eldest of five children born to a former merchant seaman and his schoolteacher wife. Wallace was a bright, literate child, with a genuine appetite for adventure. His mother would always say this was his father's influence. Wallace was so used to being the master to his siblings at home that he grew into a confident and competitive young man. The Campbell family read and discussed the *Book of Common Prayer* and were actively involved in the church. Wallace appreciated how faith formed a bond with his family and the community. He also liked the sense of order.

For a short time he had considered entering an Anglican seminary, but instead chose to pursue those literary passions—until he met and married the ravenously beautiful Anna. Twelve short months later, the arrival of a baby greatly blessed them. They named him James. There were no more thoughts of either the seminary or writing. Wallace took a position teaching literature at All Souls Secondary School in the rustic manufacturing city of Coventry in the West Midlands. Outside the city center, their modest home was a short bicycle ride from the school.

Wallace, like many Britons, had hoped that England could stay out of the war. He had too many friends who had lost fathers, uncles, and brothers in the Great War. But when the Nazis invaded Poland and Great Britain declared war in September 1939, the call of duty—of risky adventure—weighed heavily upon him. His mother encouraged him to avoid the sea and enlist in the RAF; she had lost two brothers at the Somme and was sure that her son would be safer far above the wretched earth.

Like all the other young brides, Anna was dutiful, but terrified of his possible death. He would join the RAF and signed up in January 1940.

After undergoing tests and a medical examination, Wallace enlisted as a pilot in training. At the Babbacombe Theatre Training Center in Devon, he absorbed RAF instruction that included intense physical training accompanied by classes in mathematics, navigation, and Morse Code. Although he was, as always, a talented student, he found the act of actually flying a plane to be far more challenging than he could have dreamed. His first flight was as a passenger, and aside from the exhilaration of being untethered among the clouds, Wallace was thoroughly convinced that he would never be able to master the seemingly endless number of skills necessary for successfully piloting a heavy bomber.

However, he quickly learned that flying by the gauges was quite easy. What really made a pilot ready for combat was the ability to fly by the seat of his pants, to feel the craft, to execute loops and rolls without referring to the airspeed indicator. He corroborated this challenge when one of his training mates, on his first solo, slammed mid-air into another trainer, killing himself and two others. After several grueling months, Wallace earned his wings and eventually found himself at the helm of a Lancaster, delivering payloads of bombs into France and Germany.

Even the best trained crews were at the mercy of the enemy. Their risk of being shot out of the sky was more than 40 percent, a death rate that made every flight—and airman—facing a sudden end to life on every mission.

Wallace knew the odds of survival were slim each time he took to the sky. When he thought about it, he just hoped the end would be fast and painless. For comfort, he always flew with the photo of the beautiful Anna and a smiling James attached to the control panel. This night, more than one hundred Lancasters rumbled through the darkness. The hum and vibration of the Merlin engines was numbing—the frozen air pinched his skin above his oxygen mask. Their mission was to destroy rail networks in and around Berlin.

It was Wallace's training, not fear, that kept him stoic as he watched the planes around him progress toward tonight's target. As he could not hear their Merlins over his own, they seemed to float beside him, bobbing silently up and down. Inside those Lancasters were his friends, his countrymen—all like him—all convinced they would be the ones that would return home this time. Many would not.

Wallace focused on the white contrails streaming from the aircraft around him. The contrails were winsome, lighting up the opaque blue winter sky—but they all knew, if this art continued to paint the night sky over Germany, it would only help the searchlights and enemy antiaircraft gun crews get a fix on their targets.

Wallace kept a soft grip on the throttle of *Lady Orchid* that jutted from a pedestal between him and his old chum, flight engineer Oliver Brannan, sitting in the jump seat beside him. Wallace and his mates had been through hell on over twenty missions. They were still in the sky. Before being retired from bomber flying assignments they had to complete ten more missions. To Brannan and other young crew members, twenty-eight-year-old Wallace exuded a calm and steady presence. He had to. He was their anchor, their salvation. A Lancaster had one pilot. His calm was their calm. His orders were, without question, their orders. His survival was their survival.

Wallace glanced out the frosty cockpit windows to see the squadron of fighter escorts pulling back from the convoy, lacking the fuel range to provide cover all the way to Berlin. Now the bombers were on their own, hurtling toward the air combat maelstrom that awaited them.

Flying at 15,000 feet and cruising at 280 miles per hour, Wallace saw the countryside somewhere west of Berlin below him. It was brown farmland dotted by snow. *My, how peaceful*, thought Wallace. Then he felt Oliver poking at him.

Breathing into his oxygen mask, Oliver reported, "Number 3 engine is running rough."

Wallace nodded. "Right, been feeling the shimmy. Let's not worry. Not losing any air speed. If need be, we'll shut number three down after we lighten our load on those damned Nazi rail yards and turn for home."

Oliver tried to rein in his anger. "Okay, sir. But still, it irritates me. More than once, I've told the bloody ground crew that number three likes to act up! I keep asking the bums to take her apart and replace the old gaskets. It's just ridiculous!"

"Not surprised," Wallace said. "We know that *Lady Orchid* is worn down, but she's been a faithful bird. Once we're back on base and have gotten some rest, I'll insist upon a complete overhaul."

"Good luck with that, sir."

Right behind Wallace, separated by a black screen, sat twenty-one-year-old Harold Murray, a studious lad from Blackburn, northern England. As *Lady Orchid's* navigator, he was pouring over his maps, gauges, and logbook.

"Position, Harry?" asked Wallace. "I know we're getting close."

"Yes, sir…. Just ten minutes out. Right on schedule."

Wallace felt the familiar tightening in his stomach. He glanced at the photo of Anna and James, held his breath, then exhaled. He would now focus on remaining calm in his determination to complete the mission and get his crew home safely. He knew these men would do their job. Some would say that good luck had followed them on their missions. Unlike so many other crews, now dead and gone, they had emerged largely unscathed…albeit with a few minor wounds, but with nothing close to a fatality.

Wallace always prayed for God's protection and blessings as they entered a bombing run. Up ahead, he could see the Pathfinder planes starting to drop flares over their target. Those flares were also a different signal. Soon they would be running through bursts of metal flack that could blow them out of the sky.

Wallace remembered his version of Psalm 23: "Even though we walk through the Valley of Death, we shall fear no evil; We know You are with us."

Soon lightning-like explosions and percussive booms from ground fire would buffet *Lady Orchid*, causing precipitous pitches and dips. Getting ready, Wallace tightened his grip on the wheel, steadying the plane, to begin a descent into the bombing run.

As *Lady Orchid* began to level out at its assigned bombing altitude, Wallace could see the *Just Jane* on his right and the *Growling Pluto* on his left—each illuminated in the dark night by white-hot blasts of light coming up from the ground below.

Crewmen in all the ships steadied themselves against the rolling turbulence caused by German flak. They had been through worse. Upper turret gunner Freddie Richmond, not yet twenty-years-old, coolly checked his two Browning machine guns and ammo supplies, ready for the likely Luftwaffe attack. Tail gunner Tommy O'Malley, a compact sparkplug of a man, steadied himself on what for all the world looked like a modified bicycle seat wedged into the turret at the stern of the craft. He was double checking to make sure that his four Brownings were ready to fire.

Liam "Smiley" Smithson, the radio operator, was sitting right behind the navigator. As the plane shook, he and Harry glanced nervously at each other, even as Smiley signaled Freddie with thumbs up, letting him know of his readiness to assist at the upper turret if needed.

Lying prone in the plane's plexiglass nose cone, directly below Wallace and Oliver, was bombardier Charlie "Dead Eye" Maxson. He was alert and ready when his GEE-H radar instruments told him to release the bombs. Once this critical assignment was over, he was responsible for aiming and firing the two Browning machine guns sticking out of the nose turret. That Charlie was still alive after many Luftwaffe encounters was its own kind of a miracle.

Every member of the crew was aware that the German Air Force, with all of its air losses and, more recently, fuel shortages, was still a dangerous animal. Battered and almost beaten, the Luftwaffe still had enough ME-109 and FW-190 fighters to attack and destroy some of these Lancasters.

Worse yet, the new ME-262 jet planes might show up and quickly add to wiping out these lumbering bombers. The Lancasters were particularly vulnerable to demolition, especially with no fighter plane escort protection, even as they slowly turned for their home bases in England after completing their bombing runs.

"Thirty seconds to target," came Harry's metallic voice over Wallace's headset, tone measured and precise. "Twenty-five."

Wallace checked his gauges. Steady. Level. Plenty of fuel.

As ack-ack explosions flashed to the left and right of the bombers, the next twenty seconds seemed to move at half speed. Then.....

"Let 'em go!" Harry yelled.

Dead Eye, a whippet-thin young man from Barrow, flipped the switches on the bomb release mechanism. "Away!" he barked into his headset. Holding his breath, he kept peering through the bombsight, then saw distant puffs of gray that silently erupted 10,000 feet below. "Looks like a pretty accurate hit!"

Wallace allowed himself a tight smile of satisfaction. They had made it this far. Now they would have to get home. A fresh wave of flak rocked the squadron, lighting up the night sky. As Wallace began to bank the *Lady Orchid* to the left, he felt a slam on the starboard side.

"Oliver, report."

A ball of orange and yellow mushroomed on *Lady Orchid*'s Number 3.

"We're wounded, sir! Losing power on number three."

Wallace glanced to the right through his iced windshield. Off the starboard wing *Just Jane* was in flames. Groaning, *Just Jane* began to plummet downward and to the right into the darkness. *Dammit! Pull out Teddy, pull out....*

Wallace had known Flight Captain Teddy Russell since Babbacombe. Teddy was a quiet, witty chap. He would not comment on much, but when he did his wry humor would deliver some thoughtful insight—often in the form of a pun. Wallace did not know much about Teddy, but he always liked him. Teddy was from Kidderminster—not so far away from their airbase. He and Wallace had talked about getting together sometime. Teddy never mentioned his folks or any woman. Wallace didn't ask. But now, that was that. *Godspeed Teddy. I hope you find peace soon.*

Just Jane cascaded downward and disappeared from sight.

"Snappers! Three o'clock!" Freddie shouted into his headset.

"Four o'clock low!" Tommy screeched from the rear turret.

"More, seven o'clock!" Oliver yelled.

ME-109 and FW-190 fighters were descending on the Lancasters in a swarming, lethal haze.

Harry, Freddie, and Tommy all fired. A storm of .50 shells traced through the night toward the German planes. One Focke-Wulf exploded as the shells tore the plane apart, and a second streamed thick, black smoke as it careened out of Wallace's view.

The Germans fired right back, above, below, behind. Wallace focused on turning *Lady Orchid* toward the northeast. A plodding Lancaster would be no match in a dogfight.

Wallace spoke calmly into his microphone. "Hang on, gentlemen. You know the drill. Corkscrew maneuver coming. Get ready to dance all over the sky. Let's lose these Nazi buggers."

"They're bloody everywhere!" Freddie roared as Wallace saw an ME-109 screaming toward them. Even as Freddie squeezed his trigger, a hail of bullets shredded *Lady Orchid*'s fuselage, also peppering Tommy O'Malley's turret, spraying it with a shower of his blood.

"Call in!" Wallace bellowed over the noise and confusion. Then a new sound arrested his attention, a chorus of piercing whines. Wallace looked through the plexiglass and saw two of them bearing down on *Lady Orchid* like meteors. *ME-262 jets. Flying around us like we're standing still.*

While Allied scientists and engineers devoted their attention to developing the atomic bomb, Hitler's Nazis focused their brain power on constructing missiles and jet aircraft. The result was that by the end of the war, the Germans had key technology of the future at their disposal—but not the atomic bomb. Much faster and more heavily armed than anything the Allies had available, the ME-262 was nearly unstoppable. The ever delusional Hitler had another reason to believe, even at this late date, superior technology might well mean victory for the Third Reich.

Charlie and the wounded Tommy tried to fire on the jets, but couldn't get a lock on them. A fresh rain of German bullets perforated *Lady Orchid*'s skin. Number 3 started screeching. It belched out a cloud of black smoke and quit. The ship lurched sideways. They were losing power, but Wallace was more determined than ever. He pulled hard on the throttle, anything to get out of the merciless ME-262 fire. No response.

"Oliver," Wallace shouted to his engineer right next to him. "The electronics!" Still nothing. Wallace pulled with all his might; the throttle wouldn't budge.

Freezing air whistled through the gaping holes in *Lady Orchid's* side. Wallace couldn't see much of anything, even as the undying shriek of the two German jets deafened him.

"Oliver!" Wallace glanced to his side just long enough to see why his engineer wasn't responding. His mate was hunched over into the dashboard, his eyes wide open. Blood was streaming from a gaping head wound. His body was partially blocking the throttle. What Wallace could see was the altimeter swirling, showing the plane's rapid descent. *Bloody hell! Damn you!* he thought. For a split second, Wallace was angry with everything and everyone. Including God. But then, he snapped back into the moment. *What now? No way around it. We're going down.*

As *Lady Orchid* descended toward earth, the ME-262s lost interest and turned their destructive speed elsewhere. Wallace looked through the bullet-riddled windshield and could see the dense, dark, snow-covered forest moving up toward him. The altimeter showed them passing below 5,000 feet.

"Prepare to ditch!" Wallace screamed into his headset, not sure how many more of his crew, like Oliver, were seriously wounded or dead. Through the smoke, the shattered windshield, and the deafening whine of his dying craft, Wallace could now see the specific features of individual trees, rock-filled clearings speckled with snow.

"Check in!" Wallace needed to know who was still alive.

"Navigator, check."

"Bombardier, check."

"Radio, check."

"Tail Gunner, check. I'm hit, sir. I'm bleeding but just need to be sewed up. I'll be okay."

Silence.

"Top Gunner, check in."

Silence.

"Freddie?!"

Wallace had his roster. "Okay, lads! Brace!" Wallace kept pulling on the steering mechanism with all his strength. Nothing. No response.

Wallace had once heard that most people die with a surprised look on their faces. He recalled a time when the idea of death terrified him, but now, with all that had happened back in Coventry, he was prepared for the moment with equanimity. It wasn't that he wanted to die—life still had its pleasurable aspects—it was just that he no longer clung to it the way that he once had. He reckoned that the end was marked by oblivion or perhaps the transition to another form of being. He reached for the photo of Anna and James and put it in his top left pocket.

The prospect of death didn't matter to him one way or the other anymore. He'd often consoled himself with the idea that he wouldn't even be aware of his death when it occurred. Either a black curtain fell, or maybe a reunion with all those he had loved and lost.

Still, he wasn't about to let his crew perish without pouring the very last measure of his strength. Again, he pulled back on the stick. He felt a snap. The steering column moved back. Wallace pushed hard on the throttle. *Lady Orchid* dipped low enough to practically brush the tree-tops...she finally began to level out...and slowly gain altitude.

All Wallace could hope for was that his plane would hold together long enough to get back to base. He shut down Number 2 to help balance the ship's slow forward movement. He could not relax until seeing his landing strip back in England.

Harry, Liam, Charlie, were all waiting for him when he deplaned. Tommy was sitting in a jeep as a driver put it into gear and sped off. His right arm was bloodied and wrapped in bandages.

Not much was said. They all were thinking of Oliver and Freddie. Wallace waited for the ground crew medics who would bring the two dead men off the ship. They had not survived when passing through the Valley of Death.

Wallace walked around *Lady Orchid* surveying the damage. Would she fly again? He was doubtful, but did not know for sure. He looked up toward the cockpit and said out loud, "Thank you, ma'am."

Half asleep as he sat shirtless on an examining table in the stark, utilitarian RAF Station Fulbeck hospital in Lincolnshire, Wallace was vaguely cognizant of the first light of dawn illuminating the drawn blinds in a window that overlooked the landing strips. Other than that, he felt almost numb, the pervasive ache in his gut squeezed out the possibility of any other emotion.

"No broken bones, no sign of internal injuries," said the young combat medical technician, gently palpating Wallace's belly and checking his eyes with a piercing pen light. "Looks like you'll survive, Captain," he added in a valiant attempt to be reassuring.

"How's my crew?" Wallace asked, already aware that whatever news the CMT had to share was likely not good.

"Two dead, sir...well, you know that. Very sorry about that. The rest...shaken and bruised. Rough flight. They're grateful to be alive."

The CMT saw the emotional pain register on Wallace's face. Trying to be reassuring again, the CMT said: "From what they said, it's a miracle you got anyone home in one piece. They told me the plane was falling apart when you landed it. Apparently the ship is completely beyond repair."

Wallace's eyes bored into the gray linoleum floor. "Two really good young men are gone...." He looked to the CMT. "Guess we have different ideas about what constitutes a miracle."

Wallace stood, wincing, grabbed his shirt and began putting it on.

"Sir, I really wouldn't advise...."

Before he could finish, Wallace was past him and moving through the door leading into an adjacent hallway. He approached a blonde nurse, one of many medical personnel already busy at this early hour. "Excuse me, can you tell me where...?" Behind her, he saw a sign with an arrow indicating that the morgue was down the hall to his right. "Never mind, ma'am. I see where to go. Thank you."

He made his way through shrouded forms on gurneys, haggard doctors wearing scrubs stained with red, and nurses clasping the hands of ashen-faced men praying for miracles of their own. He pushed open a pair of heavy swinging doors and found himself entering a cold, sterile, gray room. The preternatural quiet was like that of an empty cathedral.

"Sir, you're not allowed to be in here," said an attendant, who looked like he hadn't slept for days. He was walking toward Wallace, but all Wallace could see was Oliver Brannan's gray face and still open eyes staring dully at some point between him and the concrete ceiling. The right side of his face was gone. Only dried blood and brain matter was visible. The attendant moved quickly and pulled the sheet over Oliver. Wallace looked numbly at the other forms covered in white cloth, stationary ghosts on carts, waiting to be delivered to...where?

"What happens to them now?" Wallace asked quietly. "What about my turret gunner, Freddie Richmond? He was a fine lad. What about him?"

The attendant gave him a sympathetic look. "Well, sir, to be honest, there's not much left of him. The cleanup crew gathered what body parts they could find and placed them in a body bag."

Wallace just stared as the attendant said, "Come on mate, there's no point—" He saw there was no use in trying to dissuade Wallace. "We determine the cause of death. Do the necessary paperwork."

The cause of death. Torn apart. Broken. Shattered. "And then?"

"Embalmed. After that, well, local carpenters coffin up the bodies, and they're sent by railway to be taken to the RAF cemetery at Harrogate. Or home to their families when they have known loved ones."

Home. Wallace stepped toward the gurney bearing the remains of Oliver. He gently pulled the sheet back from his good friend's lifeless face. "The damn thing is, this bloody war will be over in months. Maybe weeks. That's all. Instead—" He looked around at the platoon of bodies, "this." Then Wallace gently touched his mate's shoulder and drew the shroud once again over his face. "Treat him well. He was a good and brave man."

The attendant nodded gravely. "They all are, sir."

The rising sun offered no relief from the chilling wind that blew across the tarmac as Wallace stepped outside. Not sure what else to do or where to go, pulling his flight jacket close, he reached into his upper left pocket and pulled out his photo of Anna and James. Wallace crossed to a chain-link fence at the edge of a runway. Nearby, mechanics were busy tending to planes awaiting their next mission. Their voices drifted past Wallace. He watched them for a moment—alive and even joking as they worked—and then clasped the fence and lowered his head as the tendrils of the morning fog pulled over him.

He thought to himself: *If only thy rod and staff could comfort me as we keep killing and killing…and being killed.*

YALTA CONFERENCE
February 7, 1945
Six days before the Attack

FRANKLIN ROOSEVELT, WINSTON CHURCHILL, AND Joseph Stalin had always been uneasy allies. Their bond had nothing to do with friendship, but rather, with crushing their common enemy. They met in Livadia Palace, a luxurious white granite mansion set on rolling lawns overlooking the Black Sea on the Crimean Peninsula. They had gathered to determine the distribution of territory in post-war Europe. The suspicion and distaste between West and East was palpable. The pervasive presence of armed Soviet soldiers on the grounds and surrounding the property only heightened the tension.

The three leaders met for lunch in an ornate chamber that looked into the lush Italianate courtyard. Dishes still scattered before them on the fine linen, the defeat of Hitler and his Third Reich was not a matter of doubt. It was only a matter of time. So the real question was—when?

To the east, the Soviets had taken Poland and were moving doggedly toward Berlin, kilometer by bloody kilometer. The D-Day invasion had enabled hundreds of thousands of Allied soldiers to swarm across the continent, freeing France and relentlessly pushing back the beleaguered German forces. The Ardennes Counteroffensive, well known as the Battle of the Bulge, had finally come to an end, marking Hitler's last major offensive in the western theater. Generals Dwight D. Eisenhower and Bernard "Monty" Montgomery had their troops poised to cross the Rhine River and push deep into Germany within a matter of weeks. Despite these favorable developments, Stalin remained highly distrustful of Churchill and Roosevelt, and they of him.

Stalin viewed Britain's Churchill, almost always chomping on a cigar, as a crafty and potentially devious negotiator. He feared that Churchill and America's patrician president Roosevelt, now very sickly in appearance, might negotiate their own peace settlement with Germany once Hitler was out of the way. Then they would turn their combined military forces on Soviet Russia to prevent him from securing the vital foothold in Eastern Europe that had cost his soldiers and civilians millions of lives.

Stalin, a seasoned master at literally eliminating his opposition, was not about to give up his megalomaniac's dream of an ever-expanding world order based on Bolshevik-style communism. No matter what, he expected to secure complete authority over a series of buffer states to protect the Soviet Union from the repeated incursions from the West, which had been a hallmark of Russian history from Napoleon to Hitler. That he already had his military forces in control of these territories virtually guaranteed complete Soviet domination at the war's end.

Stalin was in his usual persona—arrogant, brusque, and in a non-compromising mood. He expected more than a pledge of solidarity and support from his nominal Allies. He was demanding decisive military action from them. He was not about to let the sacrifice of so much of his country's manpower, resources, and capital be stolen from him by political double talk or backroom scheming. He would insist that the Allies draw upon their air power to help wipe out still lingering—and determined—German military resistance as Russian forces kept clawing their way westward toward Berlin, and other major cities like Dresden.

Stalin's blustering impatience was very loud and clear as he spoke through his interpreter. "Every hour we sit and eat, pose for photographs, more of my soldiers die! We have lost way too many lives.

We must end this war as quickly as possible!" spat out the interpreter, intent on adequately conveying not only the Communist dictator's words, but his emotion. "And what are you doing? The goddam Nazis are running out of fuel, supplies, and still we sit and talk!"

Roosevelt began to speak, but a fit of dry, rasping coughing—now a constant companion—cut him off. He was pale and tired, just two months shy of death.

Both Stalin and Churchill realized that he was quite unwell. They both wondered whether he would ever stop fighting, bargaining, and negotiating an end to the war until the moment of his final breath.

Finally Roosevelt's cough subsided. "And what do you propose that Prime Minister Churchill and I do?"

As leery as Stalin was of Roosevelt, he distrusted Churchill even more. He believed that the British enjoyed double-crossing their allies, which he argued they had amply demonstrated in their dealings with France and Russia during World War I. He thought of Churchill as a pickpocket who would rob a person blind for a single kopeck. It wasn't that he didn't regard Roosevelt as a lying thief as well; however, he believed that the American leader had his eye set on larger imperial coins.

"Provide evidence of the support you claim to give," said Stalin in Russian, the intermediary translating into English. "Attack key German cities from the air, disrupt their supply lines, help us finish off the minions of Hitler!"

Churchill regarded Stalin, doing his dead-level best to keep his distaste hidden. Although publicly he had extolled Stalin as being "a man of massive outstanding personality, suited to the somber and stormy times in which his life has been cast; a man of inexhaustible courage and will-power," his private opinions were anything but laudatory. Over time, he had grown wary of Stalin's single-minded lust for personal power, as well as his perpetual attempt to expand the Soviet Union. This unrelenting determination made the frowning, well-mustached Stalin a seriously dangerous political foe in the post-war world.

Ever the skilled diplomat, Churchill set aside his skeptical thoughts, took a long draw on his ever-present cigar, and asked, "What cities does the Secretary General have in mind?"

"As many as you can strike and even destroy. Chemnitz, Leipzig, and especially Dresden; my military advisers have suggested these to me," came Stalin's immediate response.

The request surprised both Churchill and Roosevelt. They didn't immediately reply. Stalin interpreted their silence as reluctance, which made his blood boil.

He clenched a fist and slammed it on the table, then unleashed a hot burst of words at the interpreter before settling his steely gaze on the Westerners.

This time, the interpreter's tone did not convey Stalin's furious bluster. The coolness in his voice was more menacing. "The Marshal has one final question. Are you committed allies of the Soviet Union or not?"

That evening, Roosevelt and Churchill convened in FDR's private apartment, the room thick with blue cigarette and cigar smoke.

"That red bastard is right on one score," said Churchill, pouring an Armenian Dvin brandy that Stalin had brought in especially for the conference. It was well-known by all attendees that Churchill always preferred a stiff drink. One of his own aides later confided that the Prime Minister had consumed "buckets" of Caucasian champagne at the meeting that would have most certainly undermined the health of any normal person. "It's long past time to disabuse Herr Hitler of any notion except that of unconditional surrender."

Roosevelt drew deeply on his cigarette, then washed the smoke down with a quaff of the brandy. Privately, Churchill worried that Roosevelt's rapidly declining health was draining the American president of his acuity, perhaps even hampering his legendary negotiating abilities to deal effectively with Stalin.

Churchill had taken note that the American wasn't as stubborn and persistent when pursuing his goals as he had formerly been. He also knew that throughout his life, Roosevelt had been, at best, lukewarm to the interests and welfare of the British Empire. Churchill feared that the political pressure Roosevelt kept facing at home to end American involvement in the war might cause the president to strike overly generous bargains with ever aggrandizing Stalin, unintentionally feeding the Soviet dictator's ravenous hunger to spread his form of communism over all of Europe—and even beyond.

Finally, Roosevelt spoke. "Our massive bombing campaigns—day and night—have not yet broken the Germans. Well, actually, the Nazis. We know Hitler will not relent. By his orders, they will keep fighting and killing. I believe we should do what Stalin has asked, attacking legitimate military targets south of Berlin from the air."

Coughing, Roosevelt stopped, gasping for breath. Finally, he continued: "You know we have good intelligence reports that Dresden, although a well-known cultural center, is the home of extensive munitions manufacturing. It's also a major railhead center with tracks being daily used to move Hitler's forces eastward in continuing to resist the Soviet advance."

"Indeed," replied Churchill. "Each day, I grimace over new reports of Hitler's V-1 and V-2 rockets flying into England, arbitrarily maiming and killing thousands of innocents. So if taking out Dresden and Chemnitz will help end this damn war, I'm all for it. And if German civilians should die, well, so be it. Sort of an eye for an eye."

Roosevelt swirled his brandy. "As long as the German people support Hitler, they're all the enemy. Regrettable, but they are not innocent. Apparently, only mass destruction will bring peace, no matter how ironic that sounds."

Churchill nodded, pleased that Roosevelt was able to see things his way.

Roosevelt stubbed out his cigarette in the well-used ashtray. "And while we launch the bombs, we will impress Comrade Stalin with our air power to help discourage any ideas he has about continuing west at war's end."

Roosevelt held up his brandy glass to Churchill, who responded in turn: "To victory, my friend."

"Yes sir, to victory," replied Churchill, "no matter how repulsive I find our dour, ever scheming, ally Stalin."

The next morning, the Communist dictator seemed to crack a smile as he reported the news to his generals. He had gotten exactly what he demanded.

GISELA
February 8, 1945
Five days before the Attack

A S GISELA AND RACHEL WEARILY trudged toward home with evening darkness enveloping them, they found themselves engulfed in the flood of people from Silesia, Poland, and Eastern Prussia—children, families, bent and gray. Gisela wondered where they would end up.

Gisela could still envision the city that she'd grown up—the spectacular Baroque gem, sparkling on the banks of the sapphire Elbe. She could still feel the warmth of her hand in her father's as they strolled through the rolling lawns of Grosser Garten, brought alive by bright arrays of impossibly brilliant displays of flowers in well-ordered beds. Sometimes they would take a carriage ride to a café, where she would eat her favorite strawberry and jelly-filled pastries while her father drank dark coffee and read the newspaper.

Even as a small child, Gisela was aware of the importance of Dresden to her family. The place where her Jewish grandparents found safety after fleeing their shtetl in the pogroms and the campaign of Jewish extermination led by the White Russians. Her grandmother Elizaveta had hidden under a woodpile when they came to kill her, only to be saved by the arrival of soldiers from the Red Army…who told her to run. There was nothing for her in Russia anymore. Somehow she and her family had escaped without starving, freezing, or being shot—like these refugees now appearing in Dresden.

Gisela remembered a city of marble fountains, immaculately manicured gardens, the stately, ancient Romanesque *Frauenkirche*, the exciting, colorful Altmarkt Square. It all seemed a lifetime ago.

"Thank you for helping save me," sighed Rachel above the tumult. "I don't know where you find the strength to go on."

"Neither do I," confessed Gisela. "But we have no choice."

Rachel regarded her close friend, admiring her resilience. Gisela had the ability to press forward when everything seemed so pointless. "Is it Jacob? The hope of seeing him again that drives you?"

The very mention of his name inspired a rush of warmth through a body that Gisela sometimes worried had lost its ability to feel. Even now, after all these horrible months, she could recall the touch of his hand on her skin, smell his hair, relax in the confidence and reassurance that emanated from him when he smiled.

She missed Jacob's eloquence, his intelligence, his stubbornness, his sense of compassion that seemed to compel him to always place the needs of others above his own. She missed the way that he was comfortable with silence, the loyalty that was an integral part of his character, the private hurts that he had endured and that he had shared only with her.

She longed to hear him sing along with her while she played the piano, his voice hopelessly and irrevocably out of tune. She ached when she remembered the long hours they had spent together laughing, loving, arguing over theology and philosophy—simply being.

Would she ever see him again? She doubted so, and yet to release the hope would be to take another tangible step toward death.

"Perhaps," said Gisela, unsure whether the flicker of hope that barely burned inside her was a beacon or delusion. "Or fighting against the admission that I never will."

Then, out of nowhere—taking Gisela by surprise—Rachel spoke in a concerned whisper. "You must get Albert to help us."

Gisela looked at Rachel as if she had just proposed they build an air balloon and fly out of Germany. "What are you suggesting?"

"You know how he's always cared for you. Use that leverage to our advantage."

Gisela still didn't understand what Rachel could possibly be thinking. "For what?"

"I don't know. Keep us safe from Gruber. Make sure they don't work us to death before rescue comes." Rachel's voice fell off. "If it ever comes."

They approached the railway station, and Gisela saw the platforms overflowing with hungry people and families. The people were not walking so much as they were shuffling along the platforms—wounded physically and spiritually, carrying their few possessions.

"You've always been the one telling me to not give up hope," Rachel reminded her.

Gisela noticed a refugee struggling to make his way through the crowd. He was unaware that some of his belongings were falling off his cart. He could not have been any older than her father, and yet he looked ancient and broken, hunched over, clothes tattered, one pant leg ripped to the knee. His beard was wispy and disheveled, his hair gray, unruly, and stuffed under a slouching woolen cap, held together by patches. Recognizing something, Gisela moved toward him, pushing her way through the throng.

Gisela picked up a blanket and then a book. As she did, a photograph fell out of its cover. Gisela knelt to retrieve it. A cottage near a field with a young couple standing at the front door, the woman in a simple wedding dress, beaming up at her new husband. On the back, a handwritten date. Just ten years earlier. She quickly replaced the photograph inside the book.

"*Herr!*" she shouted out above the din. Not surprisingly, the man didn't realize the call was directed at him. Gisela worked her way down the packed sidewalk and took him by the elbow. She handed the man his belongings.

"*Danke,*" came his weary response.

As Gisela returned, Rachel eyed the mass of humanity swarming toward the platforms as a handful of middle-aged German soldiers tried in vain to maintain some sort of order. "The trains won't hold even a fraction of those seeking passage west."

"And despite everything, they still have hope," said Gisela. "Only the will to survive keeps them going."

Rachel nodded, then looked at her friend. "Use Albert and his Wehrmacht connections."

After seeing Rachel to the rundown apartment building that she and her family now called home, Gisela made her way purposefully toward Pulsnitzer Strasse, a street known as "Judengasse" in the nineteenth century before the city council grudgingly admitted the inappropriateness of naming a street after a "religious association." Although no formal Jewish ghetto existed in Dresden, the Jewish community was now largely centered around the Jewish cemetery, the oldest in Saxony. Gisela lived there in a cramped, drafty apartment with her mother, father, and twelve-year-old brother Matthias.

Darkness came early this time of year, and this evening was unusually cold. As Gisela pulled her threadbare coat more tightly around her body, her mind momentarily flashed back to the summers she'd spent as a girl riding her bicycle with her friends, picking grapes from the vineyards dotting the slopes of the Elbe Valley near the city, then take them down to a stream, eating, laughing, lazily spending the day as only the young can do.

She recalled smelling the aster on the warm breeze, hearing the water splashing over the rocks, seeing flashes of the speckled trout just below the glassy surface. She remembered the day that Rachel felt well enough to join her and Jacob. Intrigued by the fish, she only wanted a better look. How they laughed as they pulled her from the water. She remembered Rachel's laugh as she playfully responded by pushing both of them into the stream. Such happy days were long gone.

Snapping out of her reverie, Gisela heard the coarse laughter and voices before she saw the three drunken Wehrmacht soldiers approaching her along the dark sidewalk. Like so many these days, they were little more than overgrown boys.

As early as 1943, after suffering massive losses in Russia, the Nazis had begun deploying Hitler Youth—teenage lads, sixteen- and seventeen-year-olds—directly into the heat of the fighting. Now, as a last resort, over 200,000 German boys and girls represented an important part of Hitler's forces. By 1945, the average age of all persons serving in the Wehrmacht was just sixteen years and seven months old.

Gisela believed that teenage German boys like these, despite their tough guy swagger, were usually harmless. However, these days, with the flagging war effort and the tension of what was once an unthinkable defeat looming, danger was only a careless comment or accusing glance away. She kept her eyes fixed on the pavement, attempting to project indifference and mask any hint of vulnerability.

"Look! See the yellow star. A Jewish wench!" one of them barked at her. As they moved closer, she could feel their eyes traveling over her, assessing her body.

Keep moving. Don't engage.

Her pulse quickening, Gisela didn't acknowledge them other than to glance up long enough to see a pair of red eyes leering at her. This loathsome bully moved toward her, grabbed her arm and pulled her close.

She could smell the schnapps on his breath. Then he laughed, jostling the others. "Nice looking up close. What a shame. I won't sleep with human vermin." Then he pushed her away.

Gisela allowed herself a small sigh of relief. Picking up her pace, Gisela stepped into the street to put as much distance between herself and them as possible. As she did, she heard the growl of a car engine as a large black, mud-splattered Mercedes-Benz G4 Touring Car careened around the corner.

At first she thought there was a human body tied to its bumper, but as the car roared closer, she saw it was a boar killed so recently that it still dripped crimson blood on the dark cobblestones. When the sedan rumbled past, Gisela saw a profile familiar to all Dresden Jews: that of Gauleiter Martin Mutschmann, the Nazi Regional Leader of Saxony and Dresden.

Mutschmann, age sixty-six, was an eager and dedicated Nazi, one who fully embraced the party doctrine that Marxism, communism, and Jews were the cause of all Germany's ills. He believed Jewish capitalists had been completely responsible for Germany's earlier economic difficulties. Venal and cruel, Mutschmann executed his duties with enthusiasm and relish. Still, he possessed the temerity to question human butcher and Reich Minister of the Interior Heinrich Himmler on the latter's decision to remove all Jews from German-occupied France, a grave insult to the prime architect of the Final Solution.

Not that Mutschmann cared about Jews—he personally disliked the swaggering, stuffed-shirt Himmler. He could get away with such opposition because Mutschmann remained one of Hitler's favorite regional Nazi leaders.

As Mutschmann's car receded into the night, Gisela quickened her steps toward her family's weathered apartment building with its paint peeling, windows boarded up, one edifice in a block of buildings in similar disrepair.

"Tonight we are blessed to honor the Sabbath."

Gisela stood with her parents, Hannah and Gustav, and a small group of neighbors, including Herr Victor Weinblatt, wearing a heavily worn prayer shawl, before a table bearing two nearly spent candles, a meager glass of wine, and two crusts of dark bread, covered with a well-used napkin. Her younger brother, Matthias, fidgeted with his yarmulke.

Celebrating the Sabbath at the Kauffman home every Friday night had become a comforting ritual. In these trying times, Hannah and the others found the beliefs and prayers of their Jewish faith to be more meaningful than ever.

Raised by Orthodox parents, Hannah, age forty-eight, emaciated from worry and lack of food, did her best to smile at everyone, which enhanced her matronly beauty. She still remembered how her mother and other women were confined to the upper balcony of their *schul*, while her father and the other men occupied the main floor of the sanctuary.

She recalled how excited she was the first time she was old enough to join her mother at High Holy Day services. Hannah was impressed, but also taken aback by the fervency with which her mother, dressed in a floor-length gray skirt, cried and prayed on Yom Kippur—the Day of Atonement when faithful Jews beseeched God for His forgiveness of the sins they had committed during the previous year.

That her mother had sinned at all surprised Hannah. She never remembered her mother doing bad things, but rather, regarded her as a saint who served others as a devout, principled, and caring woman. Remembering her mother in such sincere supplication affected Hannah deeply, offering a perfect role model of what she aspired to be as a loving person of good deeds, even if not as attached to the stricter principles of Orthodoxy as her parents.

As a child, Hannah enjoyed holidays like Simchat Torah because all the children received candy and fruit to remind them that God's commandments were sweeter than honey. This tradition made the almost unbearably long prayer services all worth it. She loved the rich, mellifluous baritone voice of the cantor. Her family would always walk to a nearby park after worshipping, where she would play with other children from the temple.

Hannah recalled many of her father's friends wearing elegant top hats and proudly displaying the medals that they had been awarded for serving their country in the Great War. As the political climate in Germany changed under the Nazis, fewer and fewer of these veterans displayed their medals...until none of them did at all.

In these dark days, the words of the Torah brought her comfort and reminded her of the trials that her people had endured through-out history, somehow always managing to survive. For Hannah, the Sabbath meal had always carried special meaning. It was a time every week when she could forget her troubles and immerse herself in song and poetry with her family.

The Shabbat celebration drew her particularly close to God. Hannah believed it was no accident that Shabbat was the one day of observance that was specifically mentioned in the Ten Commandments.

Even though Gisela's father Gustav was raised a Lutheran, he too wore a yarmulke out of respect to the faith of his wife and the others. At fifty, his blond hair was thinning and graying; his handsome, blue-eyed face was the source of Gisela's striking appearance.

Gustav's parents had been dismayed when he announced back in 1919 his intention to marry a Jew. Even though Hitler was still unknown, his parents were the product of a Europe that had inculcated anti-Semitic views in its people for centuries, resulting in massacres and pogroms that stretched well beyond Germany. Across the continent, Jews bore the stigma of outsiders, greedy schemers who had infiltrated banking and business. Such stereotypes ignored the truth that Jewish people chose such commercial occupations to survive, since it was illegal in many places for them to own farmland.

Generations of Europeans had grown up on and repeated anti-Semitic myths such as the misleading account that Jews had tortured and crucified a Jewish messiah who had the temerity to convert to Christianity, that Jews poisoned wells during the time of the Black Death, that their head coverings masked horns that were physical proof of their kinship with Satan.

Gustav's parents chose not to believe these stories. What they disliked was that Gustav would settle for someone of a lower station, a beautiful young Jewish woman who would not accept their Christian faith. Like the vast majority of Aryan Germans, they had done nothing to harass or harm their Jewish neighbors.

The night of Kristallnacht, November 9 to 10, 1938, upset them, but they remained silent, not protesting the mass destruction of Jewish synagogues and the random killing of various Jews across Germany. They were aware that this night of planned terror was the work of Führer Hitler and executed by Reich Minister of Propaganda Joseph

Goebbels, along with Nazi Brownshirts, SS thugs, and even members of the Hitler Youth.

The parents were not alone in passively accepting Nazi-inspired ruthlessness. Precious few Christian churches acted to defend Jews or condemn their persecution. Even though Pope Pius XII decried the Nazi notion of racial purity, the Vatican made no comment on the anti-Jewish decrees that Hitler and his minions continuously implemented.

Gustav never converted to Judaism; however, he agreed to be married in a traditional Jewish service favored by Hannah. His parents attended, under protest, as did a handful of his friends. There were other mixed marriages in Dresden, although it was rare to find a Christian man who had taken a Jewish wife.

Before the intensification of Nazi terror tactics, their marriage caused them little trouble. However, after Kristallnacht the Nazis began to separate mixed marriages into those that were "privileged" and "unprivileged," based largely on whether the couple's children were being brought up in the Jewish faith.

It was important to Hannah to raise her children according to Jewish traditions, but Gustav pointed out to Nazi bureaucrats that his children attended the local public schools. Certainly his status as a known Lutheran and respected accountant, along with his feigned Nazi Party membership, helped protect his family. Being classified as "privileged" was a godsend for Hannah, Gisela, and Matthias—at least until February 1945.

Initially, they were not required to wear a yellow star stitched into their clothing. And thus far, they had avoided the deportations to the camps that had taken away so many of their friends and neighbors, including Gisela's fiancé, Jacob. But then the day arrived when Gisela, Matthias, and Hannah had to display the *Juden* star whenever they were in public.

As they gathered for Shabbat that evening, each of them was keenly aware that the military situation had turned dramatically against the Nazis. They appreciated that Hitler's orders regarding fighting to the death were already having dire effects for Jewish spouses of German citizens and their half-Jewish children. For Hitler and his inner circle of anti-Semites, completing the "final solution" somehow remained a necessary goal, as if yet more mindless killings would appease the satanic god and magically turn the tide of war against the Allies.

Among those gathered that evening, Gisela was not alone in wondering whether there was some way to survive just long enough until the Third Reich finally collapsed. The choices were few, and they seemed to point toward failure, possibly even death. Was escape possible? Likely not, thanks to close monitoring of Dresden's streets by Gauleiter Mutschmann and his handful of Wehrmacht troops and local militia dragged into service. Besides, the refugees had inundated the local railway hubs in their frenzied flights westward from the ever-advancing Russians.

Gisela had little reason to hope, but then she recalled Rachel's advice: use Albert and his Wehrmacht connections. Then her own thought: *Perhaps before it is too late.*

Weinblatt motioned to Hannah, who stepped forward and struck a match, illuminating the faces of those gathered. "We light the candles representing the dual commandments to remember and to keep the Sabbath," he avowed. He glanced at Gisela, who stood abjectly apart from the others, her arms folded. Troubled but making no comment, Weinblatt refocused his attention on the ritual as Hannah waved her hand over the flame, then covered her eyes.

"*Barukh atah Adonai, Eloheinu melekh ha'olam asher kidishanu b'mitz'votav v'tzivanu l'had'lik neir shel Shabbat,*" she chanted solemnly.

"We light the candles to remind us that God's flame always burns within us, we gather around this table as a way to create a physical space to connect with God." Weinblatt smiled at the others.

"I feel connected," said young Matthias. "So, now can we eat?"

Gisela helped her mother ferry modest helpings of broth and meager bits of dark bread from the small kitchen as the others assembled around a table. "Unfortunately our meal isn't as sumptuous as I would like," Hannah commented. "But a secret Sabbath gathering is still possible, if we are very discrete. They haven't taken everything from us. Not yet, anyway."

Weinblatt regarded Gisela as she moved back and forth from the kitchen. "It would appear your daughter may be gravitating toward your Lutheran faith, Herr Kauffman."

"My daughter may only be half-Jewish," replied Gustav, "but her religious faith is fully that of her mother's."

The answer didn't seem to satisfy Weinblatt. "And yet she doesn't participate…." Weinblatt stopped as Gisela approached, bearing a bowl of broth.

"I meant no disrespect, Herr Weinblatt," Gisela said, moving to the table. Her tone was respectful, yet unapologetic.

"Then why didn't you join us in the prayer? It's not the first time, I've noticed."

Gisela's eyes darted toward her mother.

"You're free to speak your mind," said Hannah, while waving over Matthias's broth to cool it.

Gisela sat, taking a moment to assess her words. "I'm sorry, Herr Weinblatt, but I don't see the point in praying to a God who is silent." Gisela felt the eyes of the others focus on her. However, she didn't waver.

"And what makes you so sure He's silent?" asked Weinblatt, matching Gisela's measured tone.

"Silent. Absent. Nonexistent—call it whatever you want. We're taught that there is a covenant, but what good has it done the Jews? Now? Ever? If He won't act…what good is prayer? What good is worshipping Him? What good is He at all?"

Weinblatt sipped a spoonful of broth. "Pain, suffering, tragedy—this is the price we pay for free will. God will not and cannot interfere with history, otherwise free will would be meaningless."

"Even when free will means killing millions of innocent—"

"God has delivered us time and again."

"Tell that to Jacob! Our friends and neighbors executed at the Münchner Platz right before our eyes! The doctor who the Nazis beheaded for simply speaking the truth!" Gisela saw no point in mincing her words. "Free will. We must stand up to the devil!"

Hannah gave Gisela a stern look, and Gisela knew she had said too much. Why had she deigned to engage in this conversation at all, Gisela thought, especially on the Sabbath?

"What God does or doesn't do is not our province to question. It is why He is omniscient but unknowable. A mystery. Beyond our ability to comprehend," said Hannah.

"I'll agree with you there," replied Gisela.

"Job endured through God's silence, as did Abraham," said Weinblatt, taking off his glasses and cleaning them with the sleeve of his heavy shirt. "God does not abandon us. You should read your Torah."

"Do so if you wish, Herr Weinblatt, but I'll leave the Bible stories for the children. And put some of my faith in the Russians."

Weinblatt gave a derisive snort. "Since when are the Russians newfound friends of the Jews?"

"At least they're not sending us to death camps...."

"Not yet," Weinblatt replied sharply. Then he calmed himself.

"I had relatives who lived in Kishinev," he stated quietly. "1905. Two Russian children were found dead, and the word quickly spread that Jews had murdered them in order to use their blood in preparation of matzo for Passover. The mobs began systematically to kill every Jew in the city. Innocent people were shot, beaten to death, babies torn from their mothers' arms and smashed on the pavement. By the time night had fallen, the streets were filled with Jewish corpses. Even now, as the Soviets have taken Estonia and Latvia, they fill railroad cars with our people bound for Siberia. If not to die...."

A wave of remorse washed over Gisela; she had let her frustration and feelings of powerlessness get the better of her. "I apologize to you for saying that. Like all of us, I'm scared and don't yet see a way out from Nazi tyranny. I don't want us all to be killed," said Gisela.

Gisela's father noticed Matthias taking in her every word, deeply shaken. Gustav raised his hand to intercede. "Every day we share together is a blessing, and every day we survive is reason for hope. This family will not abandon that dream. Ever. And now, if you would all please join me."

He closed his eyes, and lowered his head, as he stood between Hannah and Gisela on either side of him. "Blessed are You, Lord our God, King of the Universe, by whose word all good things came to be."

The others said Amen.

Except for Gisela, who with her lips tight and her open eyes fixed on the bowl of broth set before her, began to consider how she might take advantage of Albert's interest in her.

ALBERT
February 8, 1945
Five days before the Attack

THE DINNER THAT ALBERT SHARED with his parents and his eight-year-old twin brothers, Rudy and Karl—though heartier than the food being eaten by the Kauffman gathering—was also less than sumptuous. Fortunately for the family, Mr. Schmidt's grocery store, the shop he had inherited from his father, allowed him to secure cheese and even the occasional bit of *teewurst* in defiance of the strict food rationing that all Germans were living under by early 1945.

The Schmidts had never had much interest in politics. However, attracted by Hitler's repeated demonization of Russia's communists, especially in reaction to their alleged burning of the Reichstag and the promise to reclaim Germany's economic prosperity, both Herr and Frau Schmidt had cast their ballots for the Nazis in the March 1933 federal elections.

Albert's father, age forty-three, considered himself a good patriot. He harbored no hatred toward Jews, and he now regularly prayed that Germany might somehow survive the war, despite Hitler's destructive madness.

"I was by the Opera House today," said Frau Schmidt, age forty-two, as she set out portions of bread, *Butterkäse*, and vegetable soup. "Refugees sleeping on the steps, seeking shelter in the alcoves. And everywhere, talk of the murderous Russians."

Rudy sat up eagerly in his seat. "I hear they will be here soon. Klaus said the communists cut off the heads of their victims and put them on spikes!" Karl, more sensitive and timid than his rowdy, athletic brother, looked nervously toward his father.

"Do you think the Russians will kill us? Karl asked. "I'm not a Nazi."

Rudy's eyes sparkled. Tormenting his brother, younger by three minutes, was one of his chief pleasures in life. "What about Albert? He wears a uniform. As for the rest of us, we're German…that's reason enough!"

Mr. Schmidt dipped a piece of bread in his soup. He admired Rudy's bright spirit and knew full well that he relished using it to cause Karl anguish. "No more, Rudy."

Rudy shot a playful glance at Karl. "It's my fault he's a pansy?" Karl's terse response came in the form of a crisp blow to Rudy's shoulder.

"Hey. No fighting at the table!" said Mrs. Schmidt as she lowered herself into her chair with a heavy sigh.

"I'm glad Hitler will not surrender," continued Karl.

Like his father, Albert considered himself to be a pragmatist. Like Karl, he was by nature a sensitive person, more enamored with literature than politics. However, he also possessed a small measure of Rudy's fire, despite his fearfulness toward combat. In his own way, he was determined to see the world return to some semblance of normalcy, no matter what loyalty oaths the Wehrmacht had required him to take or what uniform they expected him to wear.

"It doesn't matter," Albert said to Karl. "Like anyone with a brain, in public I spout the near victory propaganda that Joseph Goebbels's Reich Broadcasting Corporation promotes, but Nazi Germany will soon fall. It's inevitable. Continuing to fight will only turn our homeland into something worse than hell on earth. American and British bombs, Russian tanks—the Führer's fanaticism only makes everything worse."

Mrs. Schmidt's brow furrowed. "Albert, must we talk about these matters in front of the boys?"

"We're not babies," Rudy quickly interjected. Then, with a retaliatory shot to Karl's arm, "at least some of us."

Mrs. Schmidt turned her admonishing look on Albert. "You must keep these types of thoughts to yourself. They would not be well-received, especially from someone in your position."

They sat quietly for a moment, until Karl broke the silence. "So… if the Russians do come, what will happen to us?"

Rudy seized the opportunity to grab a piece of bread, impale it on a fork and wave it in front of Karl's face. Albert pushed his younger brother's hands away.

"There's nothing to worry about, Karl. They won't bother with children."

"And what about you?"

Albert shrugged his shoulders but showed no emotion. Rudy was not aware that he had given voice to Albert's deepest fear. He knew how vulnerable he would be if the Soviets took Dresden. As if his age and uniform weren't enough, there was the matter of his missing arm. The Russians would know how he'd incurred his wound and would certainly look to exact revenge on anyone responsible for the death of even one of the millions of their countrymen who had died in combat.

It would matter little to them that Albert had not killed anyone. His brief time at the Silesian Front had been spent keeping low, simply trying to stay out of harm's way. Albert wasn't proud of his record, but like so many other Wehrmacht soldiers, his primary mission was to keep himself alive.

The night he'd lost his arm was like a blur in his mind associated with exhaustion, cold, and ever-present fear. He had ventured behind the Russian line with an older soldier named Konrad, who, like Albert, had no desire to die for the Nazi Fatherland. Without even realizing how, they'd become separated from the rest of their patrol and found themselves clinging to the shadows in a small town whose streets were alive with Soviet soldiers. Appreciating the great jeopardy they were in by remaining in the open, they'd found an unlocked basement door beneath an abandoned house and clambered inside.

Albert's first sensation was not one of relief, but of physical illness. A warm stench emanated from the darkness. It was all that Albert could do to keep from vomiting. At that moment, they heard the thud of nearby explosions. His comrade peeked up through a basement window to see the Russians, moving systematically down the street, lobbing grenades into basements to make sure they were clear.

As Albert turned to run, his foot sank into something soft and liquid, and he pitched forward to find himself staring into the dull eyes of a corpse. As his eyes adjusted to the light, he understood the source of the sickening smell—the entire basement was littered with decaying bodies.

"Forget them," said Konrad. "We've got to get the hell out of here, or that's going to be us."

Albert realized that their only hope for escape was to head back out the door through which they'd just entered and pray to God that no one saw them.

Rifles at the ready, they charged back up wooden stairs, through the door, and into the cold night, fully expecting to be torn apart by bullets the moment they emerged. But no shots came. The patrol had crossed to the far side of the street, perhaps giving them a moment to plot their next move, perhaps about to turn and gun them down or, worse, take them prisoner.

As they crouched in the shadow of the building, gratefully gulping fresh air, Albert's comrade pointed toward an alley to what Albert guessed was east of the patrol. Albert nodded—moving in any direction was better than waiting to be seen—and they stood to run. That's when Albert saw him.

A Soviet infantryman, younger than Albert, stared fearfully at them, his breath exhaling plumes in the bitter cold air. Whether because of instinct, or training, it didn't matter, the solider pointed his PPSh at Albert. In that moment, time froze. Albert became vaguely aware of the sharp pops emanating from the Russian's gun in a wild spray, hitting nothing. Then he felt a bullet tear into his arm and looked down to see the neat hole in his sleeve at the bicep.

Albert turned his attention back onto the Soviet soldier. He watched as his companion's bullets smashed into the boy's chest and knocked him backward—instantly dead—into the snow. It was only then that the blinding pain nearly caused Albert to black out.

Konrad grabbed Albert by his good shoulder and steered him down the street toward the alley, firing blindly behind them. Somehow, Albert found the strength to run. The next few hours were nothing more than a gauzy assembly of disconnected images: breaking through a splintered wooden fence bordering what seemed to be a cemetery; running across what felt like miles of open field as rounds from a Soviet machine gun whistled past them; stumbling over the rocks in an icy stream before collapsing on a nearly frozen creek bed. Konrad beseeched Albert to stand up and keep moving, even as the rising sun illuminated a world suffused in red—then with more hands on him in a medical tent, the gaunt, joyless face of an exhausted, overworked medical service soldier suddenly asked to do the work of a surgeon.

Could a more qualified doctor have saved his arm? Perhaps, but Albert would be forever grateful that the medical service soldier, whoever he was, had saved his life. In many ways, an arm was a small price to pay for life, to be returned to Dresden from such fear and possible death. Now he wondered if it all would prove to be nothing more than a temporary reprieve. Next week, next month the Soviets might well arrive to finish the job that the young Russian soldier had begun that night on a frigid, snowy street in hell.

"If I don't offer resistance," Albert finally said, looking at his family around the dinner table, "they will certainly see that people like me were dragged into service."

Karl nodded to what was left of Albert's arm. "And how will you explain that? They'll know you fought against them."

"It only goes further to show them that I'm not a threat. The Russians won't care about me."

"And if they do? Can you escape to the west? What about all the refugees at the Opera House and the train station? You could take off your uniform, blend in with them. Get on a train and be long gone from Dresden."

Again, Albert remained impassive, but with a stab of adrenaline remembered his conversation with Rachel a few days ago. *Help us survive.* Karl's suggestion was naïve, ludicrous, completely impractical. And yet…could there be a way? Could he help Gisela? Was there a shred of possibility in this?

"Whatever happens," he said after a moment. "I'll make sure that you, everyone I care about, is safe."

Mr. Schmidt gave Karl a comforting smile. "Russians are not interested in ordinary people. We are no threat to them. We have nothing to fear."

Mrs. Schmidt gently set her spoon down and let her hands fall to her rotund belly, gently caressing it. "Enough. All this talk is upsetting the baby."

Karl brightened. "Can I touch?"

Mrs. Schmidt nodded, and Karl rested his hands on her stomach. "I can feel it!"

"Sometimes I think he or she is nothing but knees and elbows."

"Life goes on," said Mr. Schmidt reassuringly. "It always has, and it always will."

He stood and reached for the bread, allowing an envelope to fall from his sweater pocket onto the table. He looked at it quizzically. "What on earth is this?"

Rudy picked it up and looked to his father with excitement. Seeing the playful glow on Mr. Schmidt's face, he tore open the envelope and pulled out four brightly colored tickets.

"The Circus Sarrasani?" asked Karl, his voice brimming with excitement.

Mrs. Schmidt gave her husband a curious look. "How did you ever manage to—"

Mr. Schmidt made a show of grabbing the tickets back from Rudy. "You weren't supposed to see these! I'm holding them for a friend of mine. Whose children don't make fun of each other," he added pointedly to Rudy.

"I didn't tease anyone," smiled Albert, playing along.

"Very well, Albert, you can go."

"Me either!" hastily added Karl.

"You too, then. That only leaves—"

All eyes turned to Rudy. "No, please!"

Mr. Schmidt turned toward his wife. "Do you hear something?"

"Papa, I take it all back—"

"It sounds like a fly. An annoying little pest."

Albert laughed as Rudy clasped his hands and playfully begged for his father's forgiveness. However, the spark in the back of Albert's mind began grow into a small flame, increasingly demanding his attention.

At the Dresden-Neustadt train station, refugees—the more fortunate in torn, dirty coats, others wrapped in little more than rags—huddled together for warmth on the overcrowded platforms. Their tired, hungry faces were less notable than what they had collectively become: a desperate mass of humanity hoping against hope for a miracle. A few lucky ones had managed to secure tickets for the next train going west.

Albert, claiming that he'd needed to go out to meet some friends for a game of darts, stood in the shadow of a brick building in the frigid night, observing the refugees, his mind considering various possibilities. From behind, he heard approaching footsteps and turned to see a pair of young soldiers, both in their late teens, apparently on guard duty near the station.

"Heil Hitler," he greeted them.

"Heil Hitler."

Albert reached into the breast pocket of his heavy coat and produced a pack of cigarettes. He offered them to the soldiers, who nodded and pulled out a pair. As Albert struck a match, he nodded toward the miserable souls waiting for trains that now passed through less and less frequently.

"Fools. They really believe there are enough trains to take them to safety."

One of the young soldiers inhaled deeply and blew a plume of blue-white smoke into the still air. "Perhaps for those with approved travel documents. Even then…."

Albert gave a sardonic smile. "Dead already. And they don't even know it." He decided to take the gamble. "Who would even sign their papers?"

"I don't know," said the second. "Mutschmann or one of his aides, I suppose. If you have the right connections."

"Or enough money," said the first with a hard laugh.

Albert joined them as they chuckled, and then bid them a good night as they continued on.

SIR ARTHUR HARRIS
February 9, 1945
Four days before the Attack

RAF BOMBER COMMAND HEADQUARTERS, UXBRIDGE, 2:15 a.m.: Arthur Harris, age fifty-three, was sleeping fitfully, as he did most nights. Since 1942 he had served as commander-in-chief of Britain's RAF Bomber Command. By early 1945, some 50,000 of his airmen had died, with another 20,000 wounded, in the endless—and devastating—bombing raids over Germany. Many of these fallen air crews had lost their lives while serving on Avro Lancaster heavy bombers. Enemy flak, Luftwaffe fighter planes, and rarely, such accidents as crashing into one another while flying on missions, had obliterated them from the sky. Because of the hundreds of sorties that Harris had authorized, the public accorded him his popular nickname: "Bomber" Harris.

Because of these heavy casualties of the crews sent into the air, as well as persons disturbed by the millions of Germans, especially civilians, being maimed and killed during bombing sorties, persons in and out of Bomber Command had started calling him "Butcher" Harris. He knew about both names but chose not to care.

His RAF job was to crush the Hun, and he was single-minded in doing so. He believed that strategic bombing had the potential to bring a swift end to the war. He also held that Hitler's Nazi regime had earned what was coming, that the Führer was naïve to see as fair game the bombing of such cities as London, Coventry, and Warsaw and killing thousands upon thousands of civilians, but without any retribution. As Harris stated at the outset of his command, paraphrasing words from Hosea 8:7: *The Nazis had sowed the wind and were about to reap the whirlwind.*

Harris was sleeping lightly when one of his aides, a young lieutenant, started knocking on his bedroom door. The constant rapping finally woke him up, and he turned on the lamp on his nightstand. He looked at his wristwatch lying beside the lamp and observed the early morning hour.

"Yes. What is it now?" he grumbled out loud at the door.

Sheepishly, the lieutenant stepped in and saluted. He apologized for interrupting Harris's sleep, then handed him a sealed message. "From the Prime Minister, sir. Marked 'Extremely Urgent.' Your eyes only."

Harris, still not fully awake but now sitting up on the edge of his bed, stared at the envelope, then said, "That will be all."

"Yes sir," replied the lieutenant, before crisply saluting as he closed the bedroom door behind him.

Sir Arthur found his reading glasses and carefully opened the envelope. Therein he found orders about mounting a major bombing attack, one that had been discussed now and then but not yet implemented. The message had arrived from Yalta and had already received the blessing of Marshal of the RAF, Sir Charles Portal, Harris's immediate boss.

In a matter of minutes, Harris got up and dressed quickly while considering the possible size and scope of the mission.

As a high-ranking general officer, Harris had received advanced intelligence about the general purpose of the Yalta conference. Further, he was up to date on the southern thrust of the Russian advance toward eastern Germany. He suspected Stalin and his military advisers as the source of the order to take out Dresden, with the alternate targets of Leipzig and Chemnitz also approved.

Even though Harris knew that Stalin was a ruthless butcher of human beings, a part of him liked the man. After all, the Soviet high command had honored Harris in February 1944 with the rarely given medal: the Order of Suvorov First Class, awarded for his bombing efforts in support of Russian resistance efforts against Hitler's forces.

Harris did not view the Soviets as trustworthy allies, but he fully appreciated their aggressive actions along the Eastern Front as critical to winning the war. If so, helping out by bombing Dresden was a perfectly legitimate war-related action in his mind.

Since his youth, Harris had devoted his life to matters related to flight. During World War I, when primitive aircraft first engaged in aerial combat, he enlisted in the newly formed Royal Flying Corps and earned "ace" status for shooting down at least five German fighter planes. He stayed in the service after the war and kept moving up in rank while focusing on the development of more sophisticated aircraft, including heavy bombers.

Harris was among those enthusiasts who believed that strategic bombing, rather than dwelling on the fighting capacity of ground forces, could win wars simply by breaking the enemy's will to fight. Yet based on England's experience during the Battle of Britain in 1940, he witnessed that Germany's bombing of London, Coventry, and other cities had the opposite effect. The Luftwaffe's aerial attacks caused Britain's people to fight back more doggedly than ever.

By 1943, Harris could claim that his area bombing campaigns had hampered, at least in the short run, Nazi armament manufacturing and related war production. Reports, however, indicated that German morale did not appear to be dented in any significant way. Even in the carefully planned, massive, multi-night bombing campaign against the port city of Hamburg, where the death toll reached 40,000 with another 100,000 persons maimed, the remaining populace there defiantly rallied in determined support of Hitler's war effort.

Harris gathered his staff together early that morning. "Gentleman," he announced, "we have a major assignment with orders from the top... and I mean from Churchill himself, sent from the Yalta meetings."

Not known as a good listener, Harris asked for advice about shaping the plan of aerial attack. He wondered whether this operation should be as comprehensive as the devastating bombing sorties launched against Hamburg a year and a half earlier—or something more modest, yet intimidating, in scale.

"Intelligence reports greatly favor us," he stated. "The Luftwaffe in that area no longer is capable of effective resistance. Defensive ground fire will hardly exist, if at all, since the Nazis have moved aircraft weaponry once there to the Eastern front to help stop, if possible, the Russian advance."

One adviser, Colonel Henderson, spoke up in response: "Given these conditions, a more restrained bombing attack would seem to be in order, don't you agree, sir? There's no reason to kill a lot of innocent civilians."

With his eyes widening, Harris sternly replied: "Your so-called civilians, whether or not mesmerized by that SOB Hitler, keep going along with the Nazi war effort. Going along means supporting! So long as they do so, they are our enemy and will remain vulnerable to the destructive power of our bombing campaigns. Until the war finally ends, and the sooner the better, such civilians, whether guilty or innocent, will continue to die. That's the way it is in total war, like it or not."

GISELA AND HER FATHER GUSTAV
February 11, 1945
Two days before the Attack

THE SUN WOULD NOT MAKE its reluctant appearance for several hours as Gisela worked her way through the already crowded streets. The Goehle Zeiss-Ikon factory operated continuously, rotating laborers every twelve to fourteen hours, depending on production quotas. Gisela considered herself fortunate to be on the day shift, arriving at 5:30 every morning with two short ten-minute rest breaks and a half-hour midday meal break.

Laborers were to provide their own food. For Gisela that generally meant one or two pieces of half stale bread, and a bit of cheese if available. In her first days at the factory, hunger constantly gnawed at her body. Now the ever-present tightness in her shrinking stomach was—just like all the other physical and mental pain she carried—simply a mundane fact of life.

As she approached Riesaer Straße she heard commotion, shuffling feet, the bark of angry voices in the dark morning air. Then she saw a woman she knew, Frau Lieberman, stumbling toward her. She was only about fifteen years older than Gisela, but her features had been worn down into those of an elderly woman. When she saw Gisela she moved quickly, her face ashen, eyes brimming with tears.

"They came and took him. My Dieter. They took him!"

"Who took him, Frau Lieberman? Where?"

"The Gestapo. They are sending him to the Todt Brigade. The front lines. The Russians will cut him down." She grasped frantically at Gisela's sleeve. "He's only fourteen!"

The Nazis are getting desperate, Gisela thought. *Everything will keep getting worse.* Gisela sought words of comfort to impart, but they simply wouldn't come. Instead she pulled Frau Lieberman close as she sobbed.

Even Hitler's most zealous minions had to realize the end was near, Gisela surmised. *No one with Jewish blood was safe now. No one.*

The line outside Mr. Schmidt's corner grocery shop in the Altstadt area was already long, even at this hour. Gisela's father was among them. Like so many others, Gustav made it a point to arrive in the early hours of morning, hoping to be among the first to receive whatever small supplies of food Schmidt could offer.

Gustav was early enough that, near the front of the line, he was able to look through the store's front window as Schmidt bustled about inside. He saw the shelves, once filled with canned meats and fresh vegetables, cheese, bread, and noodles—now virtually bare. *Perhaps Schmidt had stores in the back and simply hadn't had the time to stock the store,* Gustav said to himself. He dispassionately noted his own optimism. *Hope doesn't die easily*, he thought, as Schmidt unlocked the front door, an hour before the posted opening time—perhaps a positive sign.

Albert's father had a warm greeting and smile for those who filed in, clutching baskets, sacks, and precious ration slips.

"Good morning, Herr Toder," Schmidt said to a man wearing a yellow star stitched to the lapel of his heavy coat as he walked back behind the counter. Gustav knew that Toder, half-Jewish, was always among the first to arrive at the store. He had five children at home, all under the age of twelve; the eldest had been stricken with polio.

Gustav watched as Toder pushed a handful of ration slips marked "Juden" across the counter. "I hope you can be generous with potatoes, Herr Schmidt," said Toder in a flat voice. "Our children are having trouble sleeping from the hunger."

Schmidt took a moment to look through the coupons. He eyed Toder, then lowered the coupons below the counter. After a moment, he lifted them back and spread them before Toder. "It appears you've come across a regular ration slip, Herr Toder. I can't imagine how such a bureaucratic oversight could have occurred."

"I can assure you, I've done nothing...."

Schmidt didn't say another word. He simply put some potatoes, a large can of herring, and some carrots and onions on the counter. Toder still didn't understand, but Gustav did. The entire world had apparently not lost its mind. Toder gathered his food and gratefully hurried away.

Gustav stepped to the counter, offered a friendly smile, and presented his coupons, two of them marked "Juden," to Schmidt. "Perhaps you can check to see if a similar error has been made in my favor."

Schmidt smiled back, collected the coupons and gave a small shake of his head. "I wish, Herr Kauffman. I wish."

The winter sun had ventured above the horizon, suffusing the streets and buildings with a soft, rosy hue by the time Gustav turned onto Pulsnitzer Strasse, clutching his canvas satchel containing the meager groceries he'd been able to obtain. As he got closer to his building, he saw the front door leading to an adjacent cluster of apartments wide open, creaking on its worn hinges in the bracing morning wind.

Then, from inside, Gustav heard the clatter of muffled crashes, angry voices—and the muted pleas of a man whose voice sounded distinctly like that of his friend, Victor Weinblatt. Gustav paused before the open door. He knew what this type of scene generally meant, and that it would undoubtedly be in his best interest to keep moving. Then came what sounded like a bookcase smashing on the wooden floor and more cries—unmistakably Weinblatt's.

Gustav was in motion before he'd even consciously decided to act. He made his way up the cramped stairway and onto a landing that served four apartments. The door to one of the units was wide open. Weinblatt's. Gustav heard glass shatter on the floor accompanied by coarse laughter and a weak groan. He pushed into Weinblatt's living room to find his friend kneeling amid shards of glass and shattered furniture.

Two young SS thugs, fresh out of the Hitler Youth and not yet twenty years old, stood before him. One of them had the barrel of his Karabiner 98k pressed into Weinblatt's cheek. Behind them, the well-fed Gauleiter Mutschmann looked on, his beady eyes conveying a clear sense of disdain and hostility.

"We know you've been leading subversive gatherings," said the young SS Nazi with the carbine. "Sowing Jewish sedition and treachery."

"No," said Weinblatt, shaking his head furiously. "The only gatherings have been to celebrate Shabbat."

The second SS tormenter raised his hand to strike Weinblatt.

"Leave him!" yelled Gustav, stepping fully into the room. He had startled the Gauleiter and his two toadies, and that was a mistake. Reflexively, the second soldier pulled his Luger from his holster and, in a single motion, smashed it across Gustav's face, driving him to the floor, knocking him all but senseless.

"Shabbat?" asked an older voice, still calm. "Are you a religious Jew? Do you believe in a power greater than you?"

Gustav was able to lift his head. Through a red haze, he saw Mutschmann kneeling by his friend. Weinblatt tried to nod, and Mutschmann gave him a tight smile. "And are you not in the presence of a greater power right here in this room? Through our god-like Führer, Adolf Hitler?"

Gustav knew that Mutschmann was, deep down, a nobody from nowhere. He was a small-minded, venal, self-centered, petty person emboldened by his Nazi uniform and his office—which made him all the more dangerous. Mutschmann had served in World War I, purportedly wounded in the line of duty. Knowing Mutschmann's character, Gustav wondered if the wound had been self-inflicted to remove himself from harm's way, although other than whispered comments there was little evidence to substantiate this rumor.

After the war, Mutschmann had managed a small lace-making business. Hard economic times that plagued everyone in Germany during the Great Depression had driven Mutschmann toward extremist, nationalist affiliations. He became an avid and active member of the *Deutschvölkischer Schutz-und Trutzbund*, a virulent anti-Semitic organization whose publications and activities helped shape the twisted racist thinking of SS Chief Heinrich Himmler, among other future German oppressors. When the Nazis began to gain prominence, Mutschmann had been an early and eager convert, organizing a local branch of the party in Plauen, located about ninety miles southwest of Dresden.

Gustav and other residents of Dresden knew Mutschmann as a vain, power-hungry man—the long since appointed Gauleiter, the regional Nazi boss of the state of Saxony. He was a skilled politician capable of extreme acts of violence and cruelty, a person who sought to exorcise his own insecurities and shortcomings through ruthless displays of power—almost always directed at those who were incapable of striking back.

Ten years earlier, he had eagerly overseen the Nazi policy of sterilizing the disabled or mentally ill in Dresden. He took great pleasure in the work.

Gustav wanted to do something to help his friend, but couldn't see clearly, wasn't entirely sure if he could even move more than an inch or two.

Again, Weinblatt nodded.

"Then pray for us," Mutschmann commanded. "In your Hebrew gibberish. So loudly they can hear you in Jerusalem!"

"You have no right," Gustav finally breathed, propping himself up. "Leave this place."

Mutschmann and the others turned their attention on Gustav. "Are you…giving us orders?"

"No. But I speak to you as a German citizen. An Aryan."

Mutschmann smirked. "You are a traitor to your race." Mutschmann eyes wandered across Gustav's groceries, now scattered on the floor among the other debris. He stooped and picked up a potato, examining it as if he'd never seen one before. "You weren't planning to share this food with your Jewish family?"

"I've done nothing wrong."

Mutschmann spotted a loaf of bread on the floor near Gustav. "That is where you are mistaken." He handed the bread to the young Gestapo enforcer, the one with the Luger. "Feed him."

The young soldier holstered his pistol, then tore off a hunk of bread. He knelt next to Gustav and began forcing the bread down Gustav's throat. Gustav tried to push him away, but his adversary was strong, and he was weak and dazed. As the boy jammed the food into Gustav's mouth, he coughed and sputtered, his heart quickly filled with dread as he realized Mutschmann's intention might well be to suffocate him. He vainly struggled but the boy shoved him back to the floor, pinning him down.

"Please," said Weinblatt, the cold barrel of the Karabiner 98k still pressed into his face.

Mutschmann seemed to be thoroughly enjoying the show. But finally his notoriously short attention span waned. Mutschmann waved his hand, and the young Gestapo released Gustav. Gustav spit out the bread, gasping for breath.

Mutschmann regarded him for a moment.

"You're fortunate I don't take a length of rope and hang you from a lamppost outside for the neighbors to see."

He squatted next to Gustav, coolly looking him in the eye. "The day of reckoning is nigh at hand." He nodded to Weinblatt. "Especially for all remaining Jews," and then, returning his gaze to Gustav, he added, "and for those who have polluted the blood of their offspring by copulating with them."

With the shuffling of boots and the slamming of a door, Mutschmann and his two SS enforcers were gone.

"Are you okay, my friend?" a very concerned Weinblatt asked, fetching a clean rag from the kitchen and pressing it gently onto Gustav's facial wound.

Gustav nodded. "And you?"

"There have been so many depredations. What is one more?"

Gustav stood, steading himself against a bookshelf that the Nazis had left standing. His face throbbed from where he had been struck with the pistol.

"For too long I've been living under the illusion that because I'm a German, a Christian, that my family would somehow be immune from all that you and others have suffered. If relief doesn't come soon...I despair for the lives of us all."

For once, Weinblatt could offer nothing in rebuttal.

WALLACE
February 11, 1945
Two days before the Attack

W ALLACE CHARGED FOR THE BALL as it bounded across the pitch. The exertion felt good, even if his lungs burned and his legs ached. Only a few years older than the others, thought Wallace, as he saw the opposing forward also closing in on the ball, but what a difference it makes. However, fueled by the fire of his innate competitive spirit, Wallace was not ready to concede anything to age just yet. He and the other man arrived at the ball nearly simultaneously. Drawing on his years as a boy in Coventry, Wallace hit the ground in a perfectly executed slide tackle, driving the ball toward a teammate and knocking his adversary to the cold, wet turf. He watched with pleasure as his side neatly passed the ball down the sideline, deep into enemy territory.

"Not bad," said the fellow from the other side as he picked himself up from the ground. "Granddad."

Wallace clambered to his feet, wiping his muddy hands on his shorts. "Caught you from behind, Sonny." Wallace jogged to the midline, trying to ignore the stabbing pain in his ribs. It felt good to escape from the real world, even for an hour, and live in a place where the only thing that mattered was putting a ball into a net.

It was then that the harsh blare of scramble klaxon cut through the chilling afternoon breeze, bringing the game to an instant halt. As Wallace put his hands on his knees and tried to catch his breath, he felt the familiar tightening in his stomach, knowing full well what the alarm signaled.

Wallace, now in uniform, found a seat near the front among other ranking field grade officers in the weathered Quonset hut that served as Fulbeck's flight briefing room. An array of flight schedules and rotations adorned the rounded, corrugated steel walls; an enormous tactical map of the European theater dominated the wall at the front of the room.

The men stood as squadron commander Colonel George Burton strode in. Wallace liked Burton. He was a tough, practical man who didn't bother with subtleties—that's what made him so good at his job. Get things done no matter the cost, and make no room for sentimentality or emotion. Not as long as there was a war on.

"Gentlemen. Be seated," said Burton with a crisp salute, taking his place at the lectern before the tactical map, spreading out papers from a manila folder. He then turned and pulled down a white projection screen from the ceiling that covered the map. Before speaking, he took a moment to collect his thoughts. Always precise, always to the point, thought Wallace. "In forty hours we are to begin a coordinated bombing attack on three targets within Germany. Chemnitz, Leipzig...and Dresden."

The mention of Dresden elicited a surprised murmur from the men. Wallace found himself speaking before he realized what he was doing.

"Dresden? Why?"

The words surprised every man in the room before falling clumsily to the floor. Burton, a stickler for procedure and protocol, looked at Wallace with a quizzical expression, not entirely sure he'd heard right. "Excuse me, Captain?"

Wallace was treading on extremely thin ice. Frankly, he wasn't sure what had possessed him to speak up at all. The men all around Wallace maintained calm expressions, but they were incredulous. There was no precedent for this sort of outburst, certainly not from Wallace—a man the others looked to as a model of calmness, professionalism, and propriety. "Why a non-military target?"

As for Burton, he couldn't contain the sudden burst of anger that flushed his face; he was stunned by Wallace's blatant insubordination. "You are wrong, Captain Campbell. Dresden is a legitimate military target with extensive manufacturing of war goods going on. The city has crucial railway connections the enemy is using to transfer troops to the east to resist the Russian advance." Burton, his pulse throbbing in his temples fixed Wallace with an iron stare, daring him to breathe another word.

Wallace understood how far he had crossed over the line. His emotional reaction and undisciplined tongue surprised him as much as it did any other man in the room. He sat back in his chair as his fellows ventured exchanged glances of disbelief.

Burton cleared his throat and referred again to his notes. He nodded to the back of the room where an aide clicked a projector that threw aerial reconnaissance images of Dresden onto the screen. "We will hit the stations. We will also target telephone systems, city administrative offices, utilities," Burton continued, his customary, controlled demeanor returning. "The attack on Dresden will be in three waves, coordinated with the Americans. The first wave will deliver explosives and incendiary devices…."

Wallace tried to concentrate on what Burton was saying, but all he could think about were those on the ground. Enemy? Perhaps. Or maybe people struggling to hang on until the damned war came to an end. Women, children, grandparents. Generally he was able to push such thoughts out of his mind, but not this time.

Thirty minutes later Wallace stood, noting that the others were reluctant to interact with him or even catch his eye. After Burton gathered his papers, he strode toward him from the lectern, still seething beneath his hard, purposeful features.

"What the hell was that all about?" Burton seethed. "Honest to God, Wallace, if it were anyone else…."

"I need to apologize, sir. I was out of line."

"Tremendously so."

The two men assessed each other. There was a great deal of shared respect, even admiration. Under other circumstances they would have undoubtedly become friends. "For God's sake, George…."

"Goddammit, we're here to do a job. No room for questions, for softness."

"Civilian targets?"

Wallace could see Burton bristle yet again. "Yes, which in coordination with the Soviet advance will inflict thousands of casualties, many of them key German personnel—"

"And thousands of them refugees and innocent civilians. God, George, you've seen the reports."

"We are RAF officers. We have our orders."

"Aye, and they're heartless orders. There must be some recourse—"

Now Burton made no effort to stem his anger. "Shall I ring bloody Harris, maybe get Churchill on the line so you can sort things out? What the hell's the matter with you?!"

"Is this what we've become, George? Marauders, butchers of women and children? The Germans are all but beaten, you know it and I know it."

"There are bigger forces at play."

"Yes. Including our humanity."

Burton was not by nature an intuitive man, but he believed he knew the reason for Wallace's reticence. "I know what it's like to lose crewmen," he said, his voice softening ever so slightly. He looked around the room to be sure that no one would overhear. "Stalin's pressuring Churchill and Roosevelt to take action, create mayhem behind the German lines in order to disrupt the Hun's troop movements eastward against the Soviets—"

"So this is politics."

"It's war."

"Bombing residential neighborhoods is a form of murder."

"As the Nazis did to us in Coventry. London—"

"—contrary to the ideals of both our nations."

"The bloody Germans have been hammered from the air for four years without any lapse of resolve or opposition to the damned Nazis. If Hitler won't surrender, what choice do we have? The goddam Nazis are deploying jets, V-2 rockets, rumors of an atomic bomb. We're airmen. The Nazi bastards won't quit. We have to beat the will to fight out of them. Even if, regrettably, civilians die. That's the reality of war."

"Words being repeated by Hitler's leaders at this very moment, no doubt. They sound no better coming from you."

Burton looked at Wallace, his anger tempered by a small measure of compassion. "God, Wallace, I would have thought you more than anyone else...."

Wallace simply shook his head. "Then you don't know me at all. When does the killing stop?"

"We deploy in forty hours. Get rested and get ready. If you choose to disobey orders, you'll face the consequences."

GISELA
February 11, 1945
Two days before the Attack

THE TIME HAD REACHED EARLY evening. Gustav had hoped that word of what had occurred at Weinblatt's apartment wouldn't circulate too widely, but in these times, in this place, such stories traveled quickly. Evidence of the brawl existed in the form of the deep gash on his forehead from the butt of the Nazi's Luger that Hannah had patiently bandaged. From what he'd learned, Mutschmann and his henchmen had made a tour of the ghetto, intimidating, invading, debasing. Something was changing, and Gustav and the others in the cold flats along Pulsnitzer Strasse and in other Jewish neighborhoods throughout Dresden could feel it.

The Nazis were growing more brazen, more frantic. *Did they really believe that victory was at hand?* Gustav asked himself. *Or were they unleashing their fury and fear on those least able to defend themselves?*

Gisela was also aware of what had happened to her father and in other similar incidents of harassment and violence across the city. Word had spread throughout the factory in frantic whispers, creating even more despair and vulnerability among the gray women who toiled there, if such a thing were possible. More than ever, she was determined to see that she and her family survived, that they would not become collateral damage as the wounded beast lashed about in the agony of its death throes.

"Gustav, the time has come," said Hannah matter-of-factly, finally breaking the grim silence that had hung over the Kauffman dinner table like a poisonous fog. "You and the children must leave."

Gisela saw Gustav's features tighten; she knew her father would never abandon her mother, which only heightened Gisela's sense of urgency to act.

"I'm the only pure Jew. It will be easier for you to get out with Gisela and Matthias."

Gustav carefully set his spoon on the table next to a bowl of broth, which he'd hardly touched. "Even if I were to consider such a thing—which I wouldn't—how would we get out? Where would we go? The train depot is jammed. The Gestapo is watching now more closely than ever."

"There are ways. To the west toward the Allies. Or even toward Portugal."

"I wouldn't think of leaving you."

"None of us would," Gisela added, resting her hand on top of Hannah's.

Hannah looked at Gisela with resigned determination. "You would if you truly loved me."

The loud knock at the front door reverberated through the small apartment like a pistol shot. Hannah looked with fear to her husband. Matthias, who had remained quiet throughout the meal, cast his eyes to Gisela. "Who do you think it is?"

Gustav made his best effort to give his son a reassuring smile. "Let's find out."

He rose and crossed to the wooden door, turning the metal lock against its objections. He opened the door to see the two young SS Nazis from Weinblatt's apartment. His first reaction was that they had come to harass his family. He thought of Gisela and the sharp knife he was fairly certain was still in the kitchen sink, awaiting washing. He would not hesitate to use it. "What do you want?" he asked, willing his voice to remain steady.

The Nazi who had smashed his face calmly reached into his coat pocket and produced a packet of papers. "Herr Kauffman. Your wife, your son, and your daughter are to report to Zeughausstrasse 1, at 06:00 hours morning after next."

"Report? For what purpose?"

The Nazi handed the papers to Gustav. "They are being removed from Dresden—by train."

A smirk pulled at the lip of his comrade. "It is for their own safety."

The words were a stab of ice to Gisela's heart. Hannah's face turned ashen. Matthias looked to them, not understanding. Gisela's only response was to hold Matthias' hand in hers.

Gustav's eyes fell to the papers. A single word commanded his attention: Stutthof.

Although the Stutthof concentration camp, in Poland east of Danzig, was not as well-known as Auschwitz or Dachau, it was the place where—during the course of the war—thousands of Jews met their death through overwork, typhus, the small but efficient Zyklon B gas chamber, or a bullet fired into the skulls of those too sick or injured to work. Doctors who worked in the infirmary at Stutthof were known to administer lethal injections to hasten the demise of prisoners who stood little chance of recovery.

The prisoners at Stutthof were used as forced labor in a variety of capacities, put to work in brickyards, food producing fields, shipyards, and even a Focke-Wulff airplane factory that had been built near the camp specifically to take advantage of the enslaved workers. As the Allies closed in on the slowly collapsing Third Reich, Stutthof was one of the last functioning Nazi concentration camps.

Mass evacuation of prisoners at Stutthof had begun a month earlier when nearly 5,000 of the camp's 50,000 prisoners were moved at gunpoint to the coast of the Baltic Seas, driven into the water, and shot. Thousands of other prisoners were marched toward eastern Germany, when their movement was cut off by the advancing Red Army. Their guards then directed them through the bitter cold and snow back to Stutthof. Many of them did not survive the journey.

As the Soviet army continued to press forward, high-ranking Nazi planners now decided to extract as many remaining Jews and half-Jews from the cities as they possibly could, assemble them at Stutthof and then put them out to sea, where they could be disposed of by drowning without danger of their bodies being discovered. It was this merciless decision that caused the Kauffmans and others throughout Germany to receive these summons, which seemed to seal their fate, even as Hitler's Aryan dream was in the process of collapsing.

The smirking Nazi looked past Gustav to the family at the table. His eyes lingered on Gisela for a moment. "Pack lightly. Don't forget your valuables," he added, with what Gisela perceived as a faint twinkle in his eye. As quickly as they had arrived, they were gone.

Gustav wandered back to the table, any pretense of putting on a brave face gone. He handed the papers to Hannah who perused them. Hands trembling, she passed them to Gisela.

"Where are we going? Will we really be safe?" asked Matthias, already sensing that they would not.

Gustav dropped his head into his hands. He didn't want his family to see the tears. Gisela, refusing to cry, pulled Matthias close.

The next knock on the door was gentler and more hesitant. This time it was Gisela who crossed to answer it. When she opened the door, she found Weinblatt and other neighbors huddled outside, pale and fearful, holding their papers.

"There is no value in killing us," said Weinblatt with genuine confusion. "We are more valuable as laborers."

Another man shook his head gravely. "I've heard the rumors. There is no more labor to be done. They are using Stutthof to gather us up and then march us to the sea or the woods where they will kill us. Those who cannot walk or become ill are shot on the spot. They are taking us in boat loads and pushing us off into the sea. I've heard the stories. Surely, you have too."

Gustav, Hannah, and the other adults sat around the Kauffman's dinner table. Gisela approached them from the hall, having finally gotten Matthias to settle down and sleep.

"Then why are they taking us there at all?" asked Rothstein, a corpulent, balding man who had been wed to a Catholic woman before she'd died earlier that winter from tuberculosis.

Gisela saw that Weinblatt was clearly a man trying to make sense of it all. "No, they need us now. To work. They still believe they can beat the Soviets," he offered weakly.

"I hate to disagree." Hannah's tone was somber yet steady. "We must face reality. This is their last chance to do away with us. Whether it's a bullet, or starvation, or drowning...."

Weinblatt looked at her with blank eyes. "So what do you suggest we do? We can't give up hope."

Hannah could only shake her head. There was nothing else they could do. Gustav rested his hand on her knee, but it brought no comfort for either of them.

Weinblatt lowered his head. "Guard us, Lord, from the hands of the wicked...." The others bowed their heads as well. "Protect us from the men of violence...."

Gisela stood, unmoving in the doorway, her eyes fully open. She wished that she could join in their prayer. But she saw no reason to do so.

Sleep did not come that night. Gisela willfully tried to set aside the fear and concentrate on what she could possibly do to save her family. There were no easy answers, no answers at all, really. But she would not go meekly, a lamb to the slaughter. It would be better for them to flee under the cover of darkness to the West. If a bullet or starvation or exposure awaited them, at least they would have died trying to do something.

Perhaps they could go to the woods and hide. It would be bitterly cold, and there would be nothing to eat, but she had heard stories of people who hid in holes under tarps during the day and went out foraging at night for potatoes or bread or whatever else they could stumble across or steal. She found the process of planning such schemes to be restful.

However, when the gray light of dawn filtered through the curtains in the window, it burned away the well-intentioned fantasies of the night and clarified the reality of the day. There were no good options. Little reason for hope.

But she silently kept thinking and vowed to keep trying.

WALLACE
February 12, 1945
One day before the Attack

"**I** WAS A SCHOOLTEACHER WHEN ALL this began. Living in Coventry. I enlisted. To defend my country, help save England." Wallace looked into the glass of whiskey before him as though it might contain an answer for the hundred questions racing through his brain. "I've flown twenty-four missions. Honorably performed my duty, regardless of how I felt. And now, once again...I'm being ordered to bomb innocents."

Wallace pursued his point in search of understanding. Listening was Patrick Hendricks, age forty-eight, who had served as an Anglican priest at Holy Trinity Church, near Coventry, before the fighting began. He'd been a boxer in his younger days—"Hammering Harry" a local journalist had dubbed him. He never dreamed of becoming a clergyman before entering Westcott House after having his nose broken and felt the calling of Christian service.

Before enlisting as a chaplain in the RAF, Hendricks's days had consisted largely of study and prayer, composing sermons, providing counseling for young couples who found marriage to be more challenging than they had expected, and organizing community teas and rummage sales. That all had changed when the German bombers first struck London in September 1940.

Hendricks enjoyed conversing with these young soldiers, but the job was far more challenging than he originally imagined. The only sense of peace he had these days came during sleep, but the first light of dawn brought with it the horrors that he had momentarily forgotten—blood, pain, death, young men in the prime of their lives who would never walk or see again. He thought that they might be considered the fortunate ones. His assignment was to provide comfort, to help them make sense of their horrible wounds, to assure them that they were in the palm of God's hands through Jesus Christ, even when staring daily into the abyss of pain and death.

"My job is not to justify the war, Wallace. I'm here to tend to the spiritual and emotional needs of men in uniform like you—soldiers who are often asked to make horrific choices and sacrifices. Let me assure you that whatever you are feeling, God feels it too."

The chaplain finished his whiskey as Wallace refilled his own glass before offering to top off Hendricks's as well. The chaplain politely waved him off.

"The Nazis can go straight to hell as far as I'm concerned." Wallace took another sip of the Jameson. "But these endless bombing runs—what's the point? Killing innocents who don't care about ideology or supremacy. People who are Hitler's pawns. Collateral damage in the pursuit of what? Endless suffering and death?"

Hendricks considered the question carefully. He lacked an easy answer. "Jesus tells us to forgive. But we are also called to battle evil."

He regarded Wallace for a moment. "I've spent time in Coventry as well; I served at a church not that far away for a short time before the war. When I think of the destruction the Nazis did with their bombs there, the hundreds of innocent lives they took...."

As soon as he saw the pain register on Wallace's face, Hendricks knew. "I'm sorry. You didn't...."

Wallace couldn't recall the last time he had shared his personal pain with anyone, much less a man of the cloth. Even after all this time, the wound was fresh, the words stuck in his throat.

"Anna and James," he said with the faintest of smiles. "My beautiful wife and my handsome young son. They were going to visit me the following week when I was on furlough. We were planning to meet in Cambridge. Visit the botanical gardens at the university, let James roam around outside. He so loved the feeling of being on his own, so long as Anna was near him."

Wallace couldn't bring himself to look Hendricks in the eye. "My son was only three."

Dropping bombs represented the first phase of Hitler's design to invade England with naval and land forces. With the British Isles neutralized and all of western Europe trapped in the Nazi's grip, the Führer then planned to turn east and invade Russia to create a dominant *Lebensraum*, or massive "living space" for his gloriously imagined Aryan nation. However, the Luftwaffe failed to soften up the British people by bombing their airfields and cities. The Blitz resulted in the loss of thousands of innocent lives in London and elsewhere, but failed to break British fighting resolve.

London took the worst of the bombings in endless attacks over several months. Coventry, a manufacturing center in the heart of England, also took a beating, the most destructive raid occurring on one horrific night in mid-November 1940. Over 500 Luftwaffe Dornier bombers pummeled the city with high explosive and incendiary bombs. The German raid leveled over 4,000 homes, destroyed two-thirds of Coventry's buildings, and killed nearly 600 people, while wounding and maiming thousands more. Dozens more lost their lives the following morning when an undetonated bomb near the Coventry and Warwickshire Hospital exploded without warning, burying people alive.

Surviving the Blitz represented a seminal time in generating united British determination to defy Hitler's inflammatory invasion plans. Prime Minister Churchill was at his best in constantly rallying the populace while offering them nothing "but blood, toil, tears, and sweat." He exhorted them to "never, never, never give up," to appreciate that "success is not final, failure is not fatal: it is the courage to continue that counts." The people listened and, like Wallace, relentlessly fought back, deeply embittered by the losses of their loved ones.

Although Wallace was not in Coventry that dreadful November night, the images that haunted him were as vivid as if he had been standing in the town center himself. He could see the buildings exploding, the chaos, fire, smoke, and rubble—dead bodies littering the streets, men, women, and children dazed and bleeding, wandering aimlessly as death rained down from above. He could hear the thunder of the 3.7-inch AA guns and 40mm Bofors firing up into the orange night sky, illuminated by the flames consuming the magnificent Coventry Cathedral.

When off by himself, he often shed tears when he imagined what it had been like for a young mother and a little boy, huddled in terror in the darkness, praying to survive before exploding Nazi bombs ended their lives. He imagined Anna cuddling James close to her, surely singing to assure him that all would be well. Her only concern, Wallace was certain, was not just for her safety as much as for the precious life of their son. When he listened closely, he thought he could hear Anna's voice above the deafening rumble: *It will all be fine. Mummy's here. It will be fine.*

But all was not fine. Not for Wallace. Most nights, even shots of whiskey didn't lessen his despair.

Ending his reverie, Wallace finally spoke. "At first, the hate fueled me. Gave me a reason to get up each morning and look forward to dropping bombs. I often imagined them blowing Hitler to bits, sending him straight to an eternity of living in hell that he so richly deserves. As time dragged on and I flew more missions, my anger and bitterness began to feel hollow, slowly disappearing. All that killing wouldn't bring Anna and James back to me. Nothing can. How destroying more civilian lives will ever satisfy anything, I don't know."

Wallace pushed his empty glass away and lifted his eyes to Hendricks. "I promised Colonel Burton to think over the matter, but in so many ways my heart tells me to refuse the assignment and admit my willingness to keep fighting is gone, whatever the consequences."

Hendricks said he understood. He explained how some friends questioned how he, a servant of God and His son Jesus Christ, could enlist and support taking up arms against his fellow human beings, encouraging men to fight and kill in the name of Britain's survival.

"In the end," he replied to Wallace, "I sincerely prayed and prayed, ever asking for God's forgiveness. My prayers and faith brought me peace. What I can say is that you must decide for yourself. Let not pain and guilt be your guide. Think of this: To save civilization, we must keep fighting until it's finally over. Please consider your choices carefully in both thought and in your prayers."

For a moment, Hendricks thought he should say no more. He offered a reassuring smile. Then he changed his mind and added: "It's not my job to convince you to keep fighting. That's up to you, your conscience, and your faith in God. But I will ask you to consider this: by helping to end this war as quickly as possible, how many lives might you save in the long run?"

Wallace shook his head.

"I really don't know. Please understand. I'm not afraid for myself. If I die, well, my prayer is to be reunited in heaven with Anna and James. But I'm also responsible for the survival of my flight crew. It's painful for me to accept their deaths, just as I viewed two of them forever dead the other morning in the morgue. I only have a few hours to decide whether to fly or stay on the ground. I just don't know."

Hendricks replied. "You're a good man, Wallace. Pray, trust God, and do as your mind and heart advise you."

GISELA
February 12, 1945
One day before the Attack

THE MACHINES AT GOEHLE ZEIS-IKON thrummed on, but Gisela and the other women at their posts felt more ghost-like than ever.

Rachel stared dully at the endless stream of parts that passed before her, her hands moving as if controlled by someone else. "Stutthof," she breathed beneath the metallic din. "No hope. It's death."

"Our people have survived for over five thousand years," Gisela replied, though the words sounded even hollower spoken aloud than they had in her mind. Still, she would not give up, but try whatever was necessary to survive. For her parents' sake. For Matthias. For the remote possibility that she might one day see her beloved Jacob again.

"I can't help wonder what difference survival would make. My heart feels dead. My mind is dead. My spirit is dead. Killed every day by seeing friends taken away by SS tormenters at night. Babies all but starving…old men shot for no reason at all, then seen hanging from lampposts. The Dresden I've loved is no more. It's like living in hell. Somehow, we must escape. I must think of something."

Gisela dared to look at Albert, Gruber, and the other guards to be sure they weren't being watched. Rachel followed Gisela's gaze and whispered, "I hope the Russians will come at any moment—and slaughter them all, every one of them, right where they stand."

"The Russians won't be here in time. And they are just as likely to rape and kill us along with them."

"Then we attack the guards," said Rachel in a whisper. "We have to devise a plan, give a signal. Rush them and tear their hearts out. They can't kill us all."

The same thought had occurred to Gisela in the darkest hours of the night. She could charm Albert, perhaps seize his weapon and turn his gun on the other guards. They would kill her....

Even alone in her room, Gisela dismissed the notion as that of a girl who had seen too many American cowboy and Indian movies.

Suddenly, out of nowhere, an agonized scream cut through the grind of the machinery. Gisela turned to see one of the women—a student friend from long ago—had her flowing brown hair caught in the press's mechanism. Like the others, factory rules required all of them to keep their hair bound in a scarf, but something had evidently gone wrong.

The machine continued to pound rhythmically, tearing the woman's scalp further away with each cycle, spewing out streams of blood. The workers flanking her stepped back, horrified by what they saw, their shrieks reverberating off the concrete walls. Even the guards were momentarily frozen by the shock of seeing the woman mauled before their eyes.

Only Gisela was in motion. As she raced toward the woman, Gruber snapped to attention, tearing his rifle from his shoulder. "Stay at your post!" he bellowed, pointing his weapon at Gisela. Albert saw what was about to happen. In an instant he had his 9mm Luger trained on Gisela as well. "Mine!"

Gisela, oblivious to both Gruber and Albert, reached the screaming woman as the machine relentlessly jerked her farther into the gears. Looking around frantically, Gisela spied a length of metal pipe leaning against the compartment housing. As she grasped it, there was a sharp crack and a bullet whistled past her ear before ricocheting off the concrete floor, leaving a small crater.

Albert was relieved; he'd missed, but his shot had come close enough to make it appear he'd intended to hit her. Gruber, however, was not the least bit deterred by such nuance. He raised his rifle and locked in on Gisela—it was his chance to kill this troublemaker. But now it was Albert in motion. Under the pretense of stopping Gisela, he deftly managed to put himself in Gruber's line of fire.

"Get out of the way!" Gruber bellowed.

Albert turned to him. "She's mine!"

At the same moment, Gisela thrust the heavy pipe into the machine works, followed immediately by a deafening grinding of gears, a shower of sparks, and a choking black cloud of acrid smoke as the press groaned and finally shuddered to a merciful halt. Conscious that Gruber was watching his every move, Albert raced up and used the butt of his weapon to push Gisela aside.

"Back, all of you!" he commanded. Working with his one good arm, Albert tried his best to extricate the collapsed woman. Ignoring Albert, Gisela and several of the other workers threw themselves into freeing the woman. When they finally got her disentangled, most of her scalp was gone. Gisela spied some rags on a ledge used for cleaning the machinery, and she grabbed them and held them to the woman's scalp to somehow stem the bleeding.

Gruber wanted to act, to shoot, but in the smoke and confusion it was impossible. He charged to where Gisela and the others were tending the falling woman. "Get away! Out! Everyone out!"

Gisela looked up at him, cradling the unconscious woman. "She's still alive, she needs—"

Without a second thought, Gruber pulled his pistol from its holster and administered a quick, decisive shot to the woman's forehead. Gisela, soaked in the woman's blood, looked at him in shock. Albert and the other women stood motionless, equally stunned.

Gruber calmly put his smoking gun back in his holster. "Out. Now. Go outside."

Ten minutes later, Gisela, Rachel, and their fellow workers were still huddled in the cold air by the loading docks, numb with shock and disbelief. Albert emerged from the factory floor, like Gisela, splattered in the dead woman's blood. His eyes met hers. Then, adopting the demeanor that his uniform demanded, he crossed to her. "Come," he said, using his lone arm to motion Gisela toward a more isolated area of the courtyard.

Rachel carefully studied them as they moved away from her and the others. *Use him.*

Under the limbs of a barren beech tree, Albert indicated for Gisela to stop, then cast a furtive glance around the courtyard, checking to be certain that no one was paying them any particular attention.

"What were you thinking?" he breathed, leaning in closer to Gisela. "You're lucky you weren't shot on the spot."

"And what was I to do? Let her die? Don't you remember her? Renate Meyer from school…before this devilish time." She decided to test the boundary of exactly how much leeway Albert would offer her. She motioned to his uniform in disdain. "Before you became this dupe to Nazism."

Albert looked at her, all pretense of being her overseer gone. "I am still the person you have always known."

In that moment of Albert's vulnerability, Gisela recognized an opportunity that might never present itself again. She didn't hesitate. "I need your help, Albert. You must know we've been summoned to Stutthof." She could instantly see that he had no idea.

"Who? When?"

"All of us, even those who are half-Jewish. Early morning, day after tomorrow, at 6 a.m. Ordered to gather at the train station. You know we will never return, Albert. This is the last chance the Nazis have to kill as many of us as they can, to hide our bodies, to conceal their murderous acts from the world. Albert, you are our only hope."

In another place, at another time, she would have felt awkward shamelessly manipulating Albert, playing on his long-standing affection for her in this fashion. But not now.

Albert's mind raced as he considered the repercussions of what she was asking. He could envision many risks. The chances of the two of them getting away alive were almost nonexistent. Far more likely was that Gisela would be murdered for being half-Jewish, and him executed as a traitor.

He was vaguely aware that she might simply be using him, that her feelings might never be the same as his—even if Jacob were dead. He also knew that as the Soviets approached from the East, getting closer by the day, the time for such audacious plans was riper than ever. The two of them might be able to get away. To make a new life. Possibly together.

"I might be able to do something. Exit documents. Signed by Gauleiter Mutschmann. Travel west by train, walk if necessary. Find Americans, British—even the French. Surrender to them."

"Can you get such papers?" Even though she had convinced herself that hope was all but gone, her heart jumped at the possibility.

Albert surveyed the courtyard again, worried that they might be overheard. He lowered his voice. "Remember Rolf from school? He's assigned to Mutschmann's office as a clerk."

Gisela could restrain her emotions no longer. "Get them, Albert! Please. For me, my mother, Matthias, Rachel, as many…."

For a moment, Albert looked at her as if she hadn't understood a word he'd said.

"Gisela. If it's even possible, if Rolf doesn't refuse or turn me in to be hanged or shot, I would lucky to get two passes. For us."

It was then that Gisela understood the price of escape.

"Albert…I can't leave my family behind."

"Don't you understand? It's your only hope."

Gisela knew he was right. If she agreed, the chance was there that she would know safety and security again, have a home, children, possibly even with Jacob, if he were still alive. Life. All hers still for the taking.

JAMES KIRBY MARTIN AND ROBERT BURRIS

"No, I can't. I can't forsake my brother and my parents. They are everything I hold dear."

Albert stood still as Gisela turned and walked away to rejoin the others. He wanted to call out to her, to beg her to change her mind, but this wasn't the time or the place. He had to face the cold reality that she really did not care for him—a wounded man, a Wehrmacht soldier, and apparently, for all she knew, a loyal devotee of Hitler.

Wordlessly, he turned and trudged back toward the factory where the mechanics were busily assessing the damage to the machines. He wanted to help Gisela, but if she wouldn't allow him to, what could he do?

Neither Albert nor Gisela realized that Gruber, who had seen to the body's removal from the building, was watching them from shadows of the factory entrance.

The only question was what he had overheard.

GISELA
February 12, 1945
One day before the attack

F OR THE FIRST TIME IN her life, Gisela couldn't envision the future. She'd always been able to imagine what the next minute, hour, or day might look like, but now it was nothing but a black void. She mourned the end of her own life, but what seemed to be inconceivable was the obliteration of her entire world. Her family, her friends. Everything they had dreamed, laughed about, argued and worried over…all wiped away, as if none of it had existed at all. That the Russians would undoubtedly arrive within weeks after everything had been destroyed was too overwhelming to think about. She knew what Jacob would say.

He would remind her that she was in God's hands, even at this moment. That even in death He would not abandon her or those who honored Him. But Jacob was also a man of action; that is what Gisela loved most deeply about him. He would tell her to embrace her grief but not to wallow in it. Instead, he would say with that ever-present fire in his eye, that she must use what she was feeling to inspire her to action. To wrestle with God, to close the gap between faith and fear by filling herself with the mettle that God had blessed her with. To be strong and courageous and know that God was with her every step of the way, never leaving or forsaking her.

She'd once felt the same way, but now…how could any of this be the plan of God? It simply made no sense. And still, she could hear Jacob's words.

As she gazed down on the empty street from her small bedroom window, she could also hear the angry voices, the crying, the shouts of protest from that cold night months before. There, below, were the ghostly images of the squad of Nazis, herding a procession of men, women, and children with yellow stars stitched on their clothing down the dark cobblestone street. That night, she had watched from above, filled with terror and anger, just as now she was consumed with sadness and futility. She'd seen the mothers holding their babies close, some wailing, others remaining stoic. Families holding hands, older siblings trying to comfort their younger brothers and sisters. Then, in the tumult, Jacob was there. Handsome, intelligent, and unbending.

As the soldiers prodded him down the street, Jacob looked back up at Gisela's window. Whether he saw her or not, she never knew. But she would always remember the determination on his face, his refusal to show fear or be dominated even as he and the others were being herded to the train station and then to the camps.

Gisela had felt compelled to charge down the stairs, fling open the front door and go to him, to use whatever influence she had as a half-Aryan to try to convince the soldiers to release him. If they refused, she thought, then she would go with him to their fate—together until the end, whatever that might mean.

For a moment, her attention was drawn to a young boy, lying in the street, crying, clinging to one of the Nazi's legs, pleading for mercy. She remembered thinking for a moment that it was Matthias, somehow caught up in the violent tide. It wasn't. The soldier kicked the boy, grabbed his collar and pulled him to his feet and threatened to shoot him on the spot if he didn't do as he was told.

Jacob had pushed his way back to the boy, scooping him up into his arms. As they melted into the frightened mass, the last image she had of Jacob was of the boy burying his face into Jacob's strong shoulder as her beloved comforted him. *Be strong. Be courageous.*

She stared out into the dark, starless night. Was it possible that her beloved was still alive out there somewhere? Was that preferable to the alternative? She tried not to imagine him, skeletal and sallow, fighting to stay well enough that he wouldn't be shot or beaten. Maybe death would have been a blessing. He would have reassured her that they would see each other again someday in *olam ha-ba*, the "world to come." Maybe he was right. She doubted it, but maybe it was true.

Gisela looked over at Matthias as he slept. Turning from the window, she drew the curtain, then crossed to her brother's bedside and knelt. As she gently brushed the hair back from his forehead, her heart filled with resolve. She would not let him pass from this world, given the remote prospect of better things to come. She would fight. She would not let her brother go with the hope of the Allies' arrival just over the horizon.

At that very moment, Mr. Schmidt lay alongside his wife in their bed, gently caressing her pregnant belly.

"The baby won't rest," she murmured. "Any time now. You will be able to get away from the store? When the time comes?"

"I don't know why I keep it open at all. There is almost no food. Soon I will only go just to turn customers away."

Mrs. Schmidt placed her hand on top of his. "I'm happy the Russians are nearly here. I don't want another of our children brought into this insane world."

"I don't know that it's ever been different. Wasn't the last war to be the one that ended all wars? And the one before that? And before that? Maybe this is the world as it really is, and our fantasies of what it should be are the illusion."

"Perhaps. But that doesn't mean that someday the dream can't come true."

The soft but insistent knock on the front door surprised them. Few would be out at this hour. Schmidt gave his wife a reassuring smile, then grabbed his robe as he swung his legs over the edge of the bed.

He opened the main door. "Gisela?" He looked both ways down the hall before quickly pulling her in, closing the door behind her. "What's wrong? It's not safe for you to be out at this hour." Schmidt could tell from her demeanor that something important had drawn her out onto the dangerous streets.

"I've come to see Albert."

Schmidt sensed a movement behind him. Albert stepped up beside him, and Schmidt understood that whatever was happening didn't involve him. He only hoped that his son wasn't allowing his heart to lead him toward grave danger. "I heard about the summons," he said to Gisela. "Your family has our prayers."

Gisela gave a small nod of thanks, and Schmidt retreated back down the hallway.

Albert studied Gisela, his heart filled with hope. She smiled winsomely at him. "We must work together," she said.

"I'll see Rolf in the morning...the moment the office opens," he replied.

He stepped toward her, tentatively opening his arm. Gisela stepped closer, allowing him to embrace her. She couldn't bring herself to look him in the eye. "Thank you. I know the risk you're putting yourself in for me. I will never forget it."

Albert had dreamed of this moment but thought it would never happen. Gisela was offering herself. To him. Now his mind would focus only on what it would take to get them out alive so that they could begin a life—some kind of life—hopefully together.

"Meet me at the Opera House around 16:00 hours. If all goes well, we can be on a train by evening time."

ALBERT
February 13, 1945
Twelve hours before the Attack

ALBERT SQUEEZED THE ROLL OF bills tucked in his pocket as he stood across the street from the Gauleiter of Saxony's head-quarters. The time was a little after 9 a.m. Through the frost-covered window, he could vaguely see Rolf going about his morning business. After his unexpected meeting with Gisela, Albert had been up all night, rehearsing what he would say until he realized that his best approach was simply to tell Rolf what he wanted. He really had little time for negotiation or for gentle persuasion. He had to speak his mind, then be ready for whatever happened, good or bad. He exhaled, and gave a last thought about the bridge he was about to cross.

Some risky actions can never be undone. Albert waited for traffic to pause. Then he stepped into the street, toward Mutschmann's office, trying to display the ease and confidence that he wished he felt.

He saluted the guards at the entrance with the usual "Heil Hitler," and they let him pass because of his Wehrmacht uniform. Once in the interior, he knocked on a closed door. The warmth in the building surrounded him like a blanket, relaxing him ever so slightly. "Come in," shouted a voice on the inside. Rolf looked up from his desk with surprise.

"Albert!"

Rolf gave a perfunctory smile, but had no idea why his old school chum would drop in unannounced. Albert, heart pounding but face calm, stuck to his plan. He saw that the door to Mutschmann's inner suite was secured, as was that of Untersturmführer Egon Blobel, Mutschmann's lieutenant, renowned and feared for the zeal he took in persecuting Jews. He relished sentencing anyone who displeased him to some awful form of death. Albert could only assume that men who would kill him without thinking would be unable to overhear the words he was about to speak.

"I'll come straight to the point, Rolf. There isn't time for anything else." Albert lowered his voice to the point that he was speaking in little more than a hoarse whisper. "Can you get me two sets of exit papers, signed by the Gauleiter?"

Rolf's first thought was that Albert must be joking. The grave look on Albert's face extinguished that possibility. Rolf exhaled, instinctively his eyes darted to the closed door.

"In theory, yes," Rolf finally whispered, "but what you're asking—"

They heard a noise emanate from Mutschmann's inner office. For a moment Rolf feared that the Gauleiter might enter without giving him the time to concoct a cover story for Albert's visit.

As for Albert, his fear was now gone. He realized that if anything went wrong with his plan, he was a dead man. All it would take was a word from Rolf, or that door to open before he'd accomplished what he'd come to do.

Albert needn't have feared, for at that moment, Mutschmann was agitatedly pacing the floor, almost shouting at his chief assistant Blobel about the Russian advance. Conversations outside his office were absolutely of no concern to him.

For a true believer such as Mutschmann, the collapse of the Third Reich was completely unthinkable. The Allies might have the upper military hand at this moment, he conceded, but these advantages were temporary. He had absolute faith in the Führer, or so he claimed, an unshakeable belief that Hitler would somehow outmaneuver his enemies and emerge triumphant. Mutschmann assured Blobel of his unwavering determination to defend Dresden and the Fatherland, just as Hitler expected of them until they had given their very last drops of blood.

With the kind of fervency that Hitler admired, Mutschmann had ruled Dresden with an iron fist, even as his resources and troop strength dwindled. He continued to tightly monitor the Jews and half-breeds under his control, a truth he made abundantly clear when just several days earlier when he had sentenced a certain Dr. Margarete Blank to death. Not by hanging, but by the guillotine. Her crime, in Mutschmann's view, was unforgivable: she had publicly voiced doubts about Germany's chances for victory, let alone survival. Perhaps worse, she was an avowed Communist.

Mutschmann used her public execution as a warning to others who might be tempted to join the resistance, engage in sabotage, or—unlikely as it was—attempt to escape from the city.

The Gauleiter crossed back to his desk and reviewed the evolving list his staff had compiled of the remaining Jews, subversives, communists, and deviants who remained in Dresden. Having many of them sent off to face the human horrors at Stutthof pleased him.

He excused Blobel, but not before saying that he wanted the streets of Dresden cleared of all non-Aryan vermin in preparation for the all-out fight against the Soviets. He tried to offer a confident smile in concluding, "I'm looking forward to the day—I'm positive it will be coming soon—when we Nazis will crush our enemies once and for all and establish the long-awaited thousand-year reign of the Third Reich."

As Rolf pondered Albert's request, the heavy door that separated them from the Gauleiter swung open. Mutschmann stepped into the room, the folder of names he'd been surveying clutched in his meaty hand. Albert's only conscious thought was the way Mutschmann exuded physical danger, much in the way that Gruber did. To merely be in their presence put one at risk. Mutschmann turned his unblinking eyes on Albert.

"Heil Hitler," said Albert with a smart salute.

"Heil Hitler," said Mutschmann, assessing him.

Albert prayed that Mutschmann wouldn't ask him any questions. He had no good explanation as to why he would be at the Gauleiter's office rather than serving at his post in the factory.

To Albert's relief, Mutschmann turned his attention to Rolf and handed him the folder. "Update this list and check it for accuracy. I want it delivered to my home this evening, no later than 18:00 hours."

"Yes sir," replied Rolf, awaiting any further directives. None came, and without a second glance at Albert, Mutschmann returned to his office, closing the door behind him.

Rolf looked back to Albert. "No. It is impossible. It would be death for both of us."

"Then we must be quick about it. I'm not leaving without them, and the longer we delay, the greater the risk becomes."

"Risk? For whom? All it would take is a word from me and you'd be standing against a wall ready to be shot dead with other traitors."

Albert looked his old friend in the eye. "I'm not a traitor. I nearly died for the cause. But it will all be over soon, and there is someone I must protect."

"There is no way to protect anyone anymore." Then, Rolf's curiosity got the better of him. "Who are the exit passes for?"

Again, Albert had no choice but to be direct. "For me. And Gisela Kauffman."

Rolf regarded him with disbelief. "Good God in Christ, you have to be joking. She's already on the list. With the other Jews. They're being sent to Stutthof."

"She doesn't have to be. She and her family were always kind to you, Rolf."

Rolf's eyes again traveled toward Mutschmann's closed door. "Not worth a firing squad. Or the guillotine for me."

Albert had one card left to play. He reached into his pocket, pulled out the rolled wad of money. "It's all I have." Albert saw Rolf's expression subtly change, looking tempted. In the uncertain days that lay ahead, people would need all the resources they could muster to survive.

"We can be sure what's coming, the war ending," Albert said, his voice low and cool. "When the Russians come—and they *are* coming—Mutschmann will be executed. It will be hell on earth for anyone who remains, particularly blue-eyed, blond-haired Aryans like us wearing Nazi uniforms. Money, food, everything will be scarce. When that day arrives, I won't be the only one on the run."

For a moment, Rolf didn't move. Albert was fully aware that anything could happen now. Rolf could order him to leave. He could pocket the money, summon Mutschmann and have Albert arrested.

Rolf, after what seemed like an eternity, reached across the desk and grabbed the money. He ruefully shook his head. "Caring about the fate of that woman. You are insane."

With another nervous glance toward Mutschmann's office, Rolf quickly tucked the money into his pants pocket, then slid open a desk drawer and pulled out a sheaf of forms. He hastily scribbled a facsimile of Mutschmann's signature in the appropriate places as he had been doing for months with Mutschmann's blessing. The important man had no time in his busy days for such trivial matters. "If you're caught, I'll deny I ever remember seeing you after our school days together. Let me mention that trains will be leaving this evening. You'll need to check the schedule. Get there plenty early to get seats or you will not be allowed on board. No overcrowding allowed."

Albert quickly took the passes, put them in his breast pocket and offered his hand to Rolf.

"Just get the hell out of here, and don't look back! Heil Hitler!"

Stepping outside into the warming morning air, unusual for that time of year, Albert breathed a sigh of relief. He had cleared the first hurdle. Who could guess how many more lay ahead?

GISELA AND ALBERT
February 13, 1945
Seven hours before the Attack

ALBERT HAD THE PASSES HE needed. He felt relaxed and ready to move forward with the escape plan. But he had forgotten about Gruber and what this Nazi fanatic might be wondering back at his post at the Goehle Zeis-Ikon plant. Not only had Gruber long since noticed Gisela's absence, but he was very aware that Albert was, likewise, missing from duty all that morning. Gruber was no quick wit, but even he thought that their mutual absence was no coincidence. He recalled their whisperings yesterday.

Back at home, Albert focused his mind on the escape plan. He would meet Gisela at the Opera House, show her the two passes, give her an update on the train schedule, and advise her to meet him at the station about an hour ahead of the 20:00 departure. Once they met, he would return home and do his best to say goodbye to his parents and brothers. No, he would not tell them what he and Gisela were about to do; instead, he would just make something else up to avoid a teary-eyed scene. Or dare he say anything at all?

As he thought through this plan, he gathered a small knapsack full of necessities: civilian clothing, maps, a small medical kit. He was not sure what to prepare for, since he could not anticipate all the challenges that the next few days would bring.

Once he rendezvoused with Gisela at the Opera House, he would return to grab the knapsack that he now placed under his bed. He decided that he would not tell his family what was happening, since informing them would only put them in greater jeopardy if questioned by local Nazi authorities.

As he reached the front door, he stood still for a moment to look around. The center of his world. The place he'd taken so many steps, where he'd gathered around the piano to sing with his family, where he'd taught the twins to play soccer when it was too cold to venture outside. He wondered if he'd ever see anything in Dresden again. Would he even be alive a day, a week, a month from now?

Albert thought about how upset his mother would be to learn that he was gone. He ached with disappointment about not being there when the new baby arrived. Again, he toyed with the idea of writing his mother a note, tucking it someplace where only she could find it. No, doing so was too much of a risk.

I must hold onto my faith that everything will work out for the best. He closed the front door behind him and willed himself not to look back. He had to focus on the present, because to make one misstep and overlook the smallest detail could spell doom for Gisela and him. He now walked purposefully in the direction of the Opera House.

The time was reaching past 14:00 hours. Albert was not the only person on the move. Gruber was also getting himself in motion, every instinct assuring him that his long-held suspicions about the one-armed Wehrmacht soldier and the half-Jewish woman were accurate. Since they were both brazen enough not to report to the factory, he was sure they were now scheming to escape from Dresden. Although they might be stupid enough to attempt to leave at night, on foot, Gruber suspected that Albert would use his military influence in some devious way to get away faster and farther by train.

Gruber couldn't be sure, but their absence had convinced him that their conversation yesterday had been about their fleeing. He felt obliged to act, so he left his post at the factory and began walking briskly along the crowded streets toward the Dresden-Neustadt train station, on full alert for either the one-armed soldier or his Jewish whore.

Gisela hurried down the crowded thoroughfare toward the rendezvous point. She made no attempt to hide or remove the yellow star on her coat. She didn't want to do anything that might arouse suspicion. She based her decision not to carry a bag holding basic necessities or more to avoid scrutiny; she was taking a desperate gamble that might or might not work, but she had to try.

Without rushing or appearing to be headed anywhere in particular, Gisela tried to breathe evenly to calm her nerves. She kept her head low, doing her best to blend in with the unending flow of refugees moving through the city.

Four blocks ahead, in the shadow of the Opera House, Albert rounded a corner, dressed in civilian clothes, the pack slung over his shoulder. He stopped and scanned the throng of humanity…Gisela was nowhere to be seen. Albert felt his stomach tighten. Had she lost her nerve? Had she decided that committing herself to his protection was not worth the price of possible freedom?

Almost desperately, Albert scanned the faces of everyone who passed by, trying to push away negative thoughts. After all this planning, she had to be there. They would make it onto a train and their passes wouldn't arouse suspicion. And soon they would be somewhere, anywhere west of Dresden.

Then he spied her, off in the distance. She was heading in his direction.

Albert allowed himself a small smile. He resisted the urge to call out to her and instead began walking toward her. Then he froze.

On the opposite side of the street, now pushing his way through the dense crowd, he saw Gruber moving directly toward Gisela, his lupine eyes having spotted her. Albert cursed himself. Why hadn't he gone directly to his post after his meeting with Rolf? He could have claimed he needed to take a cigarette break and not reappear, but Gisela's absence would have demanded an explanation to Gruber, to which he would have had no answer. Now this ruthless Nazi was moving toward his prey. Albert searched his brain for any idea of what to do.

Only a block away, Gisela raised her face and saw Albert. She let down her guard for the briefest of moments. Albert gave her the only warning he could without revealing their presence. He cut his eyes toward Gruber, who was now less than 100 feet from her and closing fast. Gisela saw him. Her heart pounding, she wheeled around and began moving quickly in the opposite direction. Maybe he hadn't seen her. She couldn't possibly stand out in the chaotic sea of faces. But Gruber had found her scent, and he intended to make the most of it.

"Halt!" he barked out above the clatter.

Gisela heard full well but kept moving. To get mixed into the mass of people surrounding her was her only hope—if somehow their numbers could block her from Gruber's presence. But he had her locked in his sight, and she was now his prey.

He pulled the Luger from its holster. "Stop! Now, or I will shoot!" He didn't give a damn about hitting innocent bystanders. In his mind, all of them were complicit in protecting her.

Gisela broke into a run, but the oncoming stream of people became a blockade. The crowd presented no such obstacle to Gruber, whose uniform was enough to send them scurrying out of his way. Brandishing his Luger also helped clear his pathway.

Pulse pounding, Albert stepped into the street and trailed after Gruber, still unnoticed, still without any idea what he should do.

Just ahead, Gisela spotted a narrow alley way between buildings. Her mind raced, now content with latching on the thinnest of options. If she could make it to the alley, perhaps there was an unlocked basement door, a wall that she could scale and then—

The sharp slap of a gunshot as Gruber fired his Luger into the air shattered any shred of hope that she could evade him. She could run, but then what? Be shot in the back? Perhaps be responsible for the deaths of others as Gruber fired away? No. There was nowhere to run. It was over. At least now death would come quickly. She had tried.

Resigned, she stopped and turned toward him. Gruber advanced, his pistol leveled at her belly. But the look on his face was not one of satisfaction, it was that of excitement—the hunt was still on.

"What is this, my Jew girl? What do you think you are doing?" he was shouting.

"I was on my way to the factory, Master Sergeant. My younger brother awoke ill, I had to…."

He waved for her to be silent. In his mind Jews were always liars. "Did you think somehow you could escape? Avoid going to Stutthof?"

He intently surveyed the crowd. "He's coming, isn't he? You're to meet him. Brunhilda and her Siegfried." Looking around but seeing no sign of Albert, Gruber returned his attention to Gisela, his eyes travelling over her body. He too saw the entrance to the alley.

"Please, sir I don't know what you might be thinking, but I can assure you I was headed to—"

Gruber had no intention of letting her complete her sentence. He grabbed her by the collar, pulled her through the crowd and deep into the alley. Gisela tried to break free, but he was too big, too strong. She saw that the alley was secluded, shrouded in early afternoon shadows lined with garbage containers along the rear entrances to stores. She was his possession now, and her only hope was that he wanted to execute her without the annoyance of witnesses.

Gruber threw her up against a cold wall. "Stop struggling, or I will blow your head off right now. No one out there will get involved."

He grabbed her even tighter. "I saw you talking with him yesterday. The traitor. Your lover. Making your plans."

Gisela shook her head. "No," she muttered, but Gruber pressed his gun hard into her temple, his free hand now squeezing her face.

"Did you think you would succeed?"

At first, Gisela had thought Gruber had pulled her into the alley so he could execute her without witnesses, without inciting a possible panic on the crowded streets. Now the look in his angry, red eyes told her that he had other things on his mind. Gisela knew if she couldn't get away from him, horrific things would happen to her before he shot her.

Using all her might, she tried to push him away; he effortlessly pressed her back against the bricks. He began to kiss her neck, then removed his hand from her face and reached up under her skirt. "Do you give favors to those who you think can help?" He reminded her of a slobbering dog with foul breath. She struggled to break free, but he had her immobilized. Then she felt his fingers invading her underwear. All but defenseless, she kept resisting.

Albert had seen Gruber push Gisela into the alley. As he prepared to go after them, he knew that he stood at yet another crossroad. Move on, perhaps save his own skin—or do the unthinkable and take on his military superior and try to free Gisela. His decision was easy.

He rushed into the alley to find Gruber pressing Gisela to the wall and fumbling with his zipper. Gisela saw Albert first. Her eyes widened. Sensing something was going on behind him, Gruber wheeled, Luger at the ready. When he saw Albert, he hissed through his teeth and immediately relaxed. "Only you, the one-armed nobody. For a moment, I thought it might be someone significant."

Albert took another step toward them.

"Don't. Halt!"

Gruber fixed him with a cold stare. "You are really going to challenge me over this Jew bitch? I don't know what you're thinking, but your life is about to become shorter than you can possibly imagine. Abandoning your post, aiding a prisoner? You think they won't put you to death this very day? How about the guillotine? Maybe I'll just kill you myself, right here and now."

Albert took another step forward.

Gruber smirked. "You? You think you can stop me? Even if you weren't a pathetic cripple, I could beat you into—"

In turning toward Albert, Gruber removed his hand from between Gisela's legs and slightly slackened his hold on her. Seizing the opportunity, she raised up and struck him with all her strength on the back of his head. Her blow, however slight, was just forceful enough to knock Gruber off-balance. He stumbled to the cobblestones.

Gisela was a blur.

She kicked him in the face, momentarily dazing him, wrestling the Luger from his grip. She pressed it calmly into the Nazi's cheek.

"Gisela...." Albert cautioned her.

Gruber glared at her contemptuously. "You would never—"

Gisela's only answer was to press the barrel of the pistol harder into his face. Gruber turned his fury on Albert. "You're willing to die for this Jew whore? Don't you see, there is nothing you can do save her. She will die, and you will be executed as the traitor you—"

The report of the Luger echoed off the cobblestones, blood and bits of Gruber's skull spraying across the wall. Then, all was silent.

Albert looked in shock at Gruber's twitching, sprawled body, blood pooling on the ground beneath his head, running in rivulets in the cracks between the stones. Gisela, although shaking, felt nothing.

She looked up at Albert, threw down the smoking Luger, then blurted out to him, "Do you have the passes?"

Stunned about what had just happened, he struggled to answer. "Yes. We must get out of here quickly and meet up later at the train station."

She agreed, although she had a slightly different plan. "Okay, now that I know for sure that you have two passes, I'll return home and gather up a few belongings...."

Albert could sense that something was tugging at Gisela. What? He couldn't possibly imagine. Stepping toward her, as if physical proximity would somehow help her understand the dire peril they were in, "Gisela, if we don't leave Dresden by this evening, we're both likely dead."

Gisela understood. "When should we meet again? I just need to know when. Where? At the train station? There's one more matter I need to take care of before leaving."

Gisela held out her hand. "I need the pass. In case we're separated or can't find each other. Because of the huge crowds hanging around the train station. Please. Trust me." She could only hope that his feelings for her would convince him to hand her the pass.

A whirlwind of confused thoughts raced through Albert's mind. *Could she possibly be deceiving me? Was this some kind of trick, a manipulation of his care and concern?*

For a moment he considered his options, along with hers. He pondered her plight. *Either leave Dresden with him or face almost guaranteed death awaiting you at Stutthof.* Gisela smiled, then gave him a brief hug.

Albert reached into his pocket and pulled out one of the exit documents. "There's a train scheduled for 22:00 hours, the last one set to leave tonight. Tomorrow, who knows if the trains will be running at all? God willing, when this last train departs tonight, we must be on board it."

"I will be there in time," she promised.

Albert leaned forward and kissed her on her cheek. Deep down, he was suspicious that she was holding back something critically important from him. He wanted to be wrong, so he gave her a reassuring look.

"If you can make it, there's even an earlier train," he said. "The schedule says it's set to depart the station at 20:00 hours. You might be able to make this one. Really, given what's happened, we need to get out of Dresden as soon as we can."

Albert looked at his watch. "It's approaching 15:00 hours. Do whatever is necessary to move quickly. We are in grave danger. Whenever you arrive, I'll be at the station waiting for you."

They turned and moved back onto the crowded street, leaving the lifeless body of Gruber prone on the wet cobblestones, his once-alert, rapacious eyes now staring blankly at nothing.

GISELA'S FAMILY
February 13, 1945
Six hours before the Attack

K NOWN AS "CARNIVAL" OR "MARDI Gras" in other parts of the world, the German *Fasching* celebration had occurred for several hundred years. Based on the German word for fasting, Fasching marked the beginning of the forty days of Lent during which Christians refrained from eating meat, dairy products, or consuming alcohol.

Some Germans believed that the name Fasching originated from the word *fasen*, meaning a "night of foolish and wild behavior." Over time Fasching celebrations became fun-filled, colorful events with people dressing up in costumes. The outfits, particularly those of devils and witches, supposedly functioned during the winter darkness to drive away evil spirits from both small towns and larger cities. Before the war and the political takeover by the Nazis, communities often held parades featuring marching bands and elaborate floats that often displayed satirical commentary about politicians and leaders.

Children looked forward to Fasching as an excuse to dress up outlandishly and parade rambunctiously through the city streets with their friends. Their parents often marked the occasion with balls and elegant parties, the last chance to consume copious amounts of food and heavy drink before beginning their fasts.

The afternoon of the first evening of Fasching, Hannah sat in the Kauffman apartment with Matthias at a small desk before a window looking out on the street. The time was around 15:30 hours, with deep shadows appearing as the winter sun lay low on the horizon.

Nearby, Gustav busied himself going through the motions of reading a week-old newspaper while smoking his pipe. They had determined that for everyone's sake—and particularly Matthias's—they would do the best they could to maintain the normal rhythms of life until early the next morning when they were to appear at the train station. They could do little else except keep praying for a miracle of divine intervention.

Matthias looked absently at the book his mother held before him. "It's a mistake to think that Huckleberry Finn is just a story about a boy having an adventure, or having his eyes opened to the evils of slavery."

From outside came a quick succession of small pops. Matthias, who had trouble paying attention under the best of conditions, was totally distracted. "Firecrackers!" he exclaimed. He stood and looked out the window as a group of children dressed as devils, wolves, and ballerinas raced past, waving iridescent sparklers that cascaded showers of gold and silver on the dark stones of the street.

"It's really about a boy deciding what kind of man he will be," Hannah persisted, still describing Huckleberry Finn. "Whether he has the courage to follow his own moral instincts even when they are at odds with the laws of his country."

Gustav glanced up from his paper, and Hannah gave him an exasperated look. She was obviously talking to empty air. Matthias was completely fixated on the bright, exciting cavalcade outside.

"In my day, boys who didn't listen to their lessons had to stay after school," said Gustav in the sternest tone he could muster. Matthias turned back and looked at his parents as if they'd both lost their minds.

"What's the point? They're taking us away." He motioned to the book. "Who cares what Huck thought or didn't think? Why does this matter? No one cares what I think."

A loud knock at the front door rescued his parents, who were unable to come up with anything resembling a satisfactory answer. Giving his wife an apprehensive glance, Gustav rose from his chair and unlocked and opened the door. There, dressed as colorful clown, stood Matthias's friend Heinz Becker.

"Can Matthias come out for Fasching? Does he have a costume?" Heinz blurted out, barely able to catch his breath from all the excitement outside.

Gustav turned back to see Matthias staring at him, eyes wide with hope. He then looked at Hannah. Why not?

"Give us fifteen minutes, Heinz," Hannah sighed. "Come in out of the cold."

A short time later, Hannah finished wrapping the last of several colorful scarves she had managed to scrounge up around Matthias's neck and arms as Gustav watched approvingly. Matthias eyed himself critically in the mirror on the nightstand next to the Kauffman's bed.

"I look like a woman who dances at the fair."

Hannah adjusted one of the scarves. "I don't see a dancer at all. I see a daring pirate who sails the coast of Africa, stealing treasure, taking prisoners, sinking ships."

Matthias brightened a little. "Have I ever killed anyone?"

Gustav nodded. "One scarf for every victim." He crossed to a bureau and picked up a container of his Hannah's makeup. He carefully etched a drooping mustache on Matthias's upper lip with one of her eyebrow pencils. He took a moment to admire his work.

"There. The face of the most merciless man on the seven seas. The very mention of your name sparks terror from Marseille to the ports of Barbados. To be honest, I'm a little frightened even being this close to you."

Matthias ventured another look at the mirror. This time he laughed at the dark, brooding visage that stared back at him. Beaming, he turned to his parents for their approval. It was almost more than Hannah could bear. She could scarcely hold back her tears. "The most fearsome buccaneer I have ever seen"—the words that Matthias wanted to hear.

"Can I go now?"

"Not too far. Home by eight."

"How will I know the time?"

"Listen for the bell tower. If it weren't for the bell tower that chimes every hour, we'd all be lost."

Gustav tousled his son's hair. How he wished they could all don costumes and run off into the night, never to be heard from again. Matthias gave them each a quick, grateful hug, then charged through the bedroom door and down the hall to reach Heinz.

Hearing the front door close, the Kauffmans crossed to the window. Below them, Matthias and Heinz emerged outside, joining a gang of other costumed children in the late afternoon sun. Laughing, they all raced away in search of fun and adventure.

Hannah could no longer hold back her emotions. Gustav, tears in his eyes, pulled his wife close. They stood, a pair of silhouettes, before the window, clutching each other desperately in the dying afternoon light, completely unaware of the storm that was gathering more than a thousand kilometers away in England.

WALLACE
February 13, 1945
Five hours before the Attack

EARLIER THAT MORNING, WALLACE MET briefly with his immediate commander, Colonel George Burton, at the latter's request. The two of them reconciled their differences, but only because Wallace admitted that his conversation with Chaplain Hendricks had persuaded him that more killing now might actually end the war faster, saving more lives in the long run.

Burton was direct: "Okay, Wallace, does this mean that you are prepared to fly, not to equivocate, rather carry out your full responsibilities and orders while in the air?"

Wallace hesitated for a brief moment, then finally said, "Yes."

Burton, raising his eyebrows, shot right back. "Sounds like some hesitation, Flight Captain. Doubt on your part? Do you really mean yes?"

Wallace tried to smile. This time he replied without hesitation. "Yes, sir! I am ready, sir."

"For your crew's sake, I sure hope so. You are one of our very best pilots with an enviable service record. Our group will be joining the second stream, up front among the lead pathfinder bombers.

Full briefing is set for 16.00 hundred hours. Be ready to act like a leader, Wallace."

Colonel Burton, as usual, entered the briefing room right on schedule. Mostly his presentations were concise and to the point. When he felt fatigue among his pilots, he offered some off-the-cuff comments. His goal was to use good news, no matter how much he might embellish the truth, to inspire newfound energy and to quiet fears about the death-defying risks every pilot in the room faced. What he would never say—but knew—was that some portion of the men he was briefing might be dead and gone by the time of his next mission gathering.

"Good afternoon, gentlemen. Are you ready to fly this evening?!"

Burton received an unenthusiastic response. "Yes, sir."

He snapped at them. "I've got some great news for you, and I expect you to shout back at me, 'Yes, SIR!'"

"YES, SIR!!!"

"And I mean great news. So here's the poop. The HUN is on the RUN, and I mean to tell you in only one direction—BACKWARDS! To prove what I'm saying, our favorite Nazi creep, you know his name, is pulling his troops back across the Rhine, out of Belgium, out of the Ardennes Forest. So it's only a matter of time until we destroy forever the murderous Third Reich!!! Don't sit there like bumps on a log. Give me some serious cheering."

The pilots looked around, when one of them blurted out: "Come on guys, let the Colonel hear it!" Even Wallace surprised himself by joining in the cheering.

When the voices began to fall silent, Burton started up again. "And I've got more news. Let me tell you the desperate Hun is in full retreat toward East Germany, in Hitler's desperate attempt to save Berlin from our advancing armies. And, farther south, some of his Wehrmacht divisions are being moved by rail from the Ardennes zone southeastward through the major rail center of Dresden. Once there, they will ride on trains from Dresden and link up with ever increasing numbers temporarily—but effectively—blocking the Russian west-ward advance. Intelligent reports indicate the Soviets are now just sixty miles east of Dresden."

A few pilots nodded yes, but one of them shouted, "Sir, spell it out!"

"Okay," replied Burton, "Here we go. Dresden is a major rail hub. There's extensive war-related manufacturing going on there. Enemy troops are stopping and briefly resting there before they proceed to the Eastern front."

Staring directly at Wallace, Burton continued: "Look, from all angles this city is a legitimate military target. It now exists to support Hitler's total war campaign. It's holding up the Soviet advance, a key to final defeat. And if civilians die because of our bombing, so be it. Many of them are aiding the enemy in the production of war goods that keep Hitler and his deluded cronies from accepting reality and ending this bloodbath."

Burton stopped talking. He went to the big board behind him and pulled up two maps, one showing the air route into Germany and the other a detailed aerial picture showing the layout of Dresden itself. He turned and explained the scope of the mission.

"The first wave of bombers will attack the city sometime after 21:00 hours. Leading the way will be eighteen Pathfinder Mosquitos dropping marker flares to illuminate the target. Right behind them will follow 254 Lancasters that will be dropping incendiaries to ignite fires along with blockbusters with the capacity to blow up whole build-ings. The first wave will also drop delayed action bombs that will help disrupt ground management efforts to extinguish the fires."

"So much for the first wave," Burton explained. "That doesn't in-volve our bomber group. Our assignment is to join, actually lead the second wave over the city. To attack three hours after the first wave has fulfilled its assignment. Our wave will include 529 bombers, dropping tons more incendiaries and blockbusters. The timing gap is important.

"When we arrive over Dresden, survivors will likely believe the attack has ended and will have emerged from their hiding places, some of them working to prevent a spreading firestorm. Our wave will make sure there's no quick recovery. Dresden will cease to exist as a manufacturing, communications, and troop staging area. Hopefully Hitler will recognize the terrible damage he has inflicted on the Fatherland and its people, and surrender unconditionally before all of Germany is a pile of ashes."

He paused, then added "Gentlemen...questions?

A pilot sitting behind Wallace spoke up. "Sir, what about the Americans? Are they getting off easy, as usual again?"

"Wrong on both counts," replied Burton. "We do area bombing at night. They do precision bombing during daylight. Their casualty rates are just as bad as ours, maybe even worse. They will be leading the third wave against whatever is left of target Dresden early tomorrow morning."

Burton scanned the room. "No more questions," he said, as he seemed to be staring directly at Wallace. "Okay, then. You have your orders. Get out there, get ready, get the job done, and get back home safely. That reminds me: don't expect much opposition from the Luftwaffe. There's not a lot left of Hitler's air force in most areas, except for protecting Berlin. The early weather reports indicate the skies should clear up over Dresden."

GISELA
February 13, 1945
Five hours before the First Attack

A S EARLY EVENING TWILIGHT STARTED to loom, Gisela kept pushing her way through the revelers, refugees, and even the Wehrmacht soldiers waiting to proceed east toward the oncoming Russians. She was now a murderer, aware that Gruber's body might be found at any moment. She felt nauseous, almost hopelessly confused. She needed to think, to decide on her actions over the next few hours, but she feared being recognized. What if Nazi authorities had learned from some unknown witness that a woman fitting her description was seen fleeing the alley? Feeling bereft and alone, she had to stop and consider the alternatives before she returned home. In front of her loomed the Grosser Garten. She walked in and found a bench in an obscure location. Sitting down, she put her head in her hands and began to sort through her options. She wanted to turn to God for advice in seeking clarity of purpose, but she had long since closed off the avenue of prayer.

Gisela just sat and stared, oblivious of time. Over and over, she kept asking herself whether she could really betray Albert. He had just helped save her life—and he clearly cared about her welfare as a victim of Nazism. Could she abandon him now, as was her original intent, and make sure that young Matthias substituted for her on the westward bound train? Then she thought about her beloved Jacob. Would she betray him, even if he were dead, if she went off with Albert? And what if Jacob was still alive? She then would have been disloyal to him.

Gisela had to make a decision but had no comforting answers. What she did have was one of the exit passes. Would it be her or Matthias on the train?

She got up, straightened out her clothing, and began walking toward her home. Out of loyalty to Jacob and concern to keep her family name alive, she had decided in favor of Matthias. She would try to avoid Albert and somehow get her younger brother on the train out of Dresden.

Walking briskly but continuously looking back to make sure that no Nazi authorities were approaching her, Gisela finally reached her family's apartment. She burst through the front door, breathing heavily from the pace of her walk, even perspiring despite the chilling temperature outside.

She shouted, "Matthias!" No answer came. She then walked into the kitchen where her parents were talking while dicing a couple of tiny potatoes for soup.

"Where's Matthias?!"

Her parents reacted calmly to the urgency of her question. "Out with his friend enjoying Fasching."

Gisela's heart sank. "No!" She looked at the clock on the shelf above the stove. Much more time had passed while in her reverie than she had realized. She had to find him quickly and get him prepared to get on the train.

Gisela seemed flustered. "When will he be back?!"

"I told him to be back by eight o'clock," Gustav replied, still wondering what was going on. "But you know how boys are, and there's no hurry, given what we are facing early tomorrow morning."

Hannah, always observant, noticed that Gisela's coat had some sort of a stain on it, almost looking like blood. She pointed and asked, "Hopefully not another problem at the factory? Which, by the way, why are you already at home, two or more hours earlier than usual?"

Gisela looked down, saw the stain, and mumbled something about one of the women getting a bad cut from the machinery. "I'll clean it up," she said.

Without another word, Gisela turned and charged up the stairs to the bedroom she shared with Matthias. She looked in a faded dresser mirror, saw the stain, and took off her coat, then rushed to the bathroom and scrubbed hard to remove the tell-tale blood.

All the while, Gisela kept telling herself: *Try to be calm. There should be enough time, but I've got to find Matthias...or he will face the death ride to Stutthof.*

She opened his dresser drawer and began pulling out Matthias' clothes. He would need something warm, something that would keep out the wet and the cold. She found a cotton carrying bag and stuffed the clothes inside. It has to be only as much as he could comfortably carry, but no more. She wished for some extra food for him to take along, but none existed.

As she rushed back down the stairs toward the front door, the bag over her shoulder, she called out to her parents. "I'm going to find Matthias. If he comes back, don't let him leave!"

The next thing Gustav and Hannah heard was, once again, the heavy slam of the door as it closed. They looked at each other, not able to comprehend Gisela's frenetic manner. However, they did know their daughter well enough to tell that whatever was going on, it was very important to her and her family.

ALBERT AND GISELA
February 13, 1945
Three hours before the attack

MR. SCHMIDT HAD LONG AGO observed that the most challenging aspect of any family outing was simply getting people
out the door. There were the inevitable forgotten jackets, overlooked
gloves, tickets left behind that nearly always necessitated them turning
back at least once after locking the front door. He sometimes mused
that the neighbors had noticed this pattern as well and made wagers
with one another on how many times the Schmidt family would return
home before departing once and for all.

One might have thought that the prospect of an evening at the circus would have been sufficient to inspire thoroughness and efficiency.
However, Schmidt noted—with no small measure of bemusement—
that it simply didn't seem to be the case. He alone stood at the doorway, coat and hat on, tickets tucked securely in his pocket, an island
of calm in the hurricane of activity that swirled around him.

"Where are the tickets?" his wife worried, pulling on her gloves.

"In my pocket," he calmly replied. "Boys! We're going to be late!"
This was not the case; Schmidt routinely told his family that they
should leave thirty minutes before they really needed to. Even then

they often found themselves racing up to the theater or school auditorium or concert hall with only minutes to spare before the performance began.

Karl charged down the hall, Rudy sauntering along behind him. "Can we wear our Fasching costumes to the circus?"

"Go like you are," Rudy offered. "Everyone will think you are a monkey." Karl took a wild swing at his brother, a futile gesture which Rudy easily dodged.

"Yes," replied Mrs. Schmidt to Karl's question about the costumes, just as the word "no" formed on Schmidt's lips. "Just be quick about it."

With that, Karl and Rudy barreled back down the hall toward their rooms, and yet again, Schmidt was glad he'd built a cushion of time into the evening.

His eye traveled to Albert, who stood in the living room. He seemed nervous, Schmidt thought, preoccupied. He could always tell when Albert had something on his mind.

"Are you sure you won't join us? I'm sure I can get an extra ticket," he ventured. "It would be wonderful to have the whole family together."

"That would be nice," replied Albert. Schmidt saw that even his efforts to appear casual and off-hand seemed forced. "I'm going to the cinema with Rolf and Pieter."

"Why? You love the circus." Mrs. Schmidt straightened her hat.

"Yes. When I was their age. You go and have a good time." Albert paused before adding, "I'll miss you." Now, both of his parents seemed sure that something was amiss. Albert had never been good at lying or putting on a false front, even when he was in grade school.

What was wrong, Mrs. Schmidt couldn't imagine. Perhaps it had something to do with a girl. Or maybe nothing more than the pull between wanting to remain a child while trying to grow into full manhood. She thought of asking, but decided to remain quiet. Instead, she simply reached out and softly stroked his cheek.

All Albert could think was, *please get out of here!* Of course he cherished every moment he had with them, especially knowing that when they walked out the door, it might well be the last time he ever saw them. However, he was also well aware that he was complicit in the killing of a Nazi officer, and even more than Gisela, his missing arm made him devilishly easy to identify.

Every minute that his family tarried increased the odds that armed men would burst through the door and haul him off to be killed. They might even think his family was somehow involved. *Just go!* Albert silently screamed through his forced smile. *We are all in greater danger than you can possibly know.*

Rudy and Karl gamboled into the entry way—Rudy dressed as a cowboy, Karl as Winnetou, the American Indian hero of Karl May's beloved series of novels. Naturally they would pick characters that would have the excuse to fight each other, Albert thought.

"Alright, let's go, go, go!" said Schmidt, vigorously clapping his hands. Rudy and Karl grabbed their coats and then headed out into the night, followed by their father. Mrs. Schmidt lingered behind. Something inside told her to reach out to Albert, ask him directly if something was wrong. But she didn't. Instead, she kissed him on the cheek and then followed behind the others, closing the door as she went.

They were gone, leaving Albert as alone as he had ever been. Even that horrible night in Silesia, he had an older comrade to help steer him to safety. Now both his life and that of Gisela's were in his hands. He comforted himself with the idea that he would do everything in his power to reunite with his family after the war had ended, but he wondered, come tomorrow's sunrise, if he might well be a prisoner or dead.

And so he stood, taking a last look around the apartment, doing his best to fight back the emotion. Once he was sure that his family was truly gone—he was quite aware of their propensity for multiple returns—he went upstairs, found the full pack stashed under his bed, and ensured that his exit pass was securely in his pocket.

For him, there would be no coming back.

After a long walk, Albert stood near the Dresden-Neustadt station, trying to remain inconspicuous, anxiously scanning the platforms filled with people, searching for Gisela's face. Now that he was an accessory to murder in addition to being a deserter and a traitor, Albert was more alert than ever. He'd heard no talk about Gruber's death, or even of the discovery of a body in an alley. He was certain Mutschmann's office had been notified and that his absence at the factory along with Gruber's death would merit, at the very least, an interrogation session. But he hoped to be miles away by then.

Albert spoke a little French and a smattering of English, perhaps enough to prevent Gisela and him from being shot on sight. In some ways, death might be better than facing the consequences for Gruber's killing. He redoubled his efforts to push all those dark thoughts away and focused on finding Gisela. *Where is she?* The next train, whenever it arrived, might well represent their final chance at survival.

At that moment, Gisela was still several kilometers away, frantically scouring the streets in hope of finding Matthias. She carefully scrutinized every group of young revelers, asked anyone she encountered if they'd seen a boy answering Matthias' description. *The damn costume is not making anything easier.* She passed under a bell tower and saw the time. She was already late in meeting Albert. To fail to do so would be to sign Matthias' death warrant; they would all be bound for the death camp early next morning.

"Matthias!" she cried out. The only response was her voice echoing back off the buildings. "Matthias!"

Ahead, a group of costumed children were trying to light a string of firecrackers, and Gisela raced toward them. Had she headed in precisely the opposite direction at that moment, she might have caught a glimpse of another group of children, a colorful pirate among them, as they made ready to light their own firecrackers.

"It's getting late. My mother will punish me," said Heinz to Matthias as one of the older boys struck a match against the rough curb.

"Suit yourself," shot back Matthias. "Tonight, I'm free. I'm never going back."

Gisela paid no attention to the distant crackle from behind her. Instead, she was filled with disappointment that none of the faces she saw in the group she'd approached were that of her brother.

MUTSCHMANN
February 13, 1945
Two hours before the First Attack

M ARTIN MUTSCHMANN, HIS GLAMOROUS WIFE Minna, and his guests had no idea of the fury headed their way as they gathered at the Gauleiter's palatial home located on the outskirts in Dresden. The Mutschmanns enjoyed throwing elaborate parties at their private residence. Minna was particularly fastidious and made sure no detail was overlooked. As a ranking volunteer in the German Red Cross, she wanted to throw a grand party to celebrate Fasching, especially so that she and her Nazi husband could make a public display of complete confidence and optimism about the future for the wealthy and powerful Hitler supporters living in and around Dresden.

Minna had insisted that everyone wear costumes and pestered her husband into using his office to acquire delicacies and drink that were extremely hard to come by. Although Mutschmann had endless problems weighing on him, he always tried to accommodate his wife, primarily because he'd learned the repeated lesson that trying to dissuade her once she got an idea was a futile activity. Further, he enjoyed having the right kind of German people at their home fawning over him, especially when they were influential bankers and business owners anxiously currying the favor of his Nazi uniform.

This night, the Mutschmanns and their guests feasted on the roast boar that he had recently killed at his opulent hunting lodge in the Tharandt forest. Besides this meat, the guests could indulge in sumptuous helpings of cheese, fruit, bread, and copious amounts of Moët & Chandon and Gewurztraminer, all to the euphonious background music of Wagner's "Siegfried Idyll for String Quartet" played by five talented musicians.

No one in this favored group needed ration cards. Like Mutschmann and Minna, none had the gaunt look of having lived on next to nothing. As favored Nazi Aryans, they were healthy in a plump sort of way, many of them looking like the well-fed Gauleiter whose loose-fitting uniform covered his well-developed stomach.

So many of Dresden's political, economic, and social elite were there to forget wartime realities and to celebrate Fasching. However, their bright costumes and mirthful demeanor could only temporarily mask the underlying tension and uneasiness that pervaded throughout the city in these darkening days.

"I've heard rumors that leaders of the high command are ready to surrender. Others, supposedly including Herr Hitler himself, are plotting to escape to Bolivia or Argentina," quietly stated a prominent businessman dressed as Napoleon, to a well-to-do banker coifed in lederhosen.

"Versailles was nothing compared to what will happen to us should we surrender this time," retorted his companion. "The Allied bastards will grind us into perpetual dust."

A cowboy nodded grimly. "Better that than the Russians. They will rape our women and execute us all."

Mutschmann tried to mask his anger as he ladled some roasted apples onto a portion of boar. He'd been increasingly aware of such talk over the past weeks and to hear it coming from his colleagues, those in high position—and favored by the Nazi regime—was particularly nettlesome. Their negativism infuriated him. Perhaps the guillotining of Dr. Blank hadn't had the salutary effect on certain segments of Dresden's population that he had hoped.

From his childhood days, the Saxon tradition of making marionettes had fascinated Mutschmann. His interest was not accidental; he was a man who enjoyed nothing more than having total control over other human beings, of having the power and position to pull their strings and manipulate them to do whatever he believed was in the best interest of the Nazi Party. Now he just wanted to banish negative comments from this evening of hearty celebration of the Fasching.

The Gauleiter invited himself to join the conversation of a small group, then announced, "We will crush the Soviets in the East. That, added with our powerful advances in the West, means our enemies don't stand a chance. The Third Reich will stand forever!"

He did not present his words as opinion, but rather as concrete, resolute fact. The Gauleiter acted as if anyone who doubted his pronouncement was not a truly loyal Nazi.

The others exchanged skeptical looks, but no one deigned to counter.

Mutschmann felt someone tap him on the shoulder. He turned around, only to find himself staring at a scantily clad women in a skimpy outfit. She was taller than Mutschmann, so he had to look up from her well-developed body to see her rosy cheeks and smiling face.

"Good evening, Gauleiter, sir," she said, with a noticeable slur which revealed she had not been ignoring the abundant supply of expensive wine. "My name is Inge. I've can't find my husband. You have really big eyes. Would you mind accompanying me around the room? I'm feeling very lonely." She then bent over, squeezed in on him, and kissed him on his forehead.

Mutschmann, forgetting about his skeptical guests, was enjoying this fleshy moment, but then he heard the voice of Minna calling his name.

"Certainly," he responded to Inge, "I'd welcome the opportunity to escort you throughout our home for the rest of the evening, but my wife is calling after me, and, well, you know...."

He glanced to his left, only to see his concerned housekeeper huddled up with Minna. His wife was trying to get his attention. His first thought was that they needed to put out more food and drink. He looked back at the buffet, the well-stocked bar. Supplies seemed more than ample. With a bit of a sigh, Minna dismissed the woman and walked toward her husband, who was quickly back-peddling from a confused looking Inge.

"My apologies, *Liebchen.* Someone named Staff Sergeant Zimmerman is here demanding to speak with you. In your study. He says it's very urgent."

"Even on a holiday, duty calls," Mutschmann declared to his guests, not attempting to hide his irritation. Most of them watched as he walked out of the main room.

Gerd Buchs had always been fascinated by radios and electronic communication. As a boy in Dusseldorf, he had built his own crystal radio, saving up for parts by doing chores at a local dairy. When the war began, he requested assignment as a radar operator, and his diligence and thoroughness impressed his superiors, earning him the rank of *Unterfeldwebel,* the equivalent of corporal.

Buchs was nearing the end of his shift at a freezing, gray concrete, antiaircraft bunker in German-occupied France near Valenciennes. It had been a routine day, like most days, with nothing of interest to report or even sufficiently occupy his time. His thoughts were of dinner and then his warm bunk, when something on one of the screens caught his eye.

He looked more closely. Could it be possible? His pulse began to race. "Oberstleutnant," he said, consciously trying to keep voice steady and calm.

The unblinking superior officer crossed to Buchs's side, also welcoming some relief from the tedium. A look at the screen banished any such feelings. He leaned in more closely, face tightening. "This has to be a mistake…." As the two men studied the amorphous cluster of white steadily moving forward toward them, they realized that this sighting was no mistake.

The Oberstleutnant, face ashen, rapidly crossed to a radio transmitter, hastily donning a pair of headphones. "Klotzsche Airfield, this is radar post 21-ZD," he spoke purposefully into a microphone. "Come in, Klotzsche. Enemy aircraft advancing from the west, current heading…."

Within minutes of receiving the transmission, Klotzsche Airfield, six kilometers north of Dresden, was alive as pilots rushed toward their briefing room. Their orders were to scramble and be ready to start their twin-engine crafts, but not to use up fuel in warming the engines until ordered to get ready for take-off. What they all knew was that aviation fuel was so scarce that they would not be able to stay in the air for more than about thirty minutes apiece.

Since Buchs and the Oberstleutnant could not be sure whether Leipzig, Chemnitz, or Dresden was the intended target, they could only declare that a massive stream of allied planes was flying toward the province of Saxony. The eighteen-heavy night-fighter Messerschmitt BF-110s, now on alert with pilots ready to start engines, sat tamely on the ground, patiently awaiting flying orders that never came.

Realizing how overwhelming the odds were for so few Luftwaffe planes to have any impact, especially with limited fuel and a huge wave of enemy aircraft headed their way, the local commander at the Klotzsche Airfield chose not to issue a command to fly.

"Pointless to respond," he said. "We'll just lose what planes we still have."

While making his decision, he called Mutschmann's office to inform whoever was on duty that a massive enemy air attack force was within an hour or so of striking at one or more of these three vulnerable urban targets in the Gauleiter's territory of Saxony.

Mutschmann strode into his book-lined library room (not that he'd read many of the books; they were mostly there for show). He was not the least bit pleased that Sergeant Zimmerman had interrupted the party, including his chat with flirtatious, more than half-drunk Inge. Zimmerman, one of his trusted staff members, was looking at a case displaying one of the Gauleiter's prized marionettes, a likeness of the devil that had been used at the Saxon Marionette Theater back in the late nineteenth century.

When Mutschmann entered, Zimmerman turned from the case and offered the standard, arm-raised salute, "Heil Hitler!"

"What is it?" the Gauleiter shouted, not bothering to return the salute.

This was how Mutschmann's life seemed to be now, every minute of every day. Yet another presumed crisis, somebody always needing something. Ordinarily he admired Zimmerman's thoroughness and attention to detail, even if the man seemed to be completely lacking in his ability to tell the difference between genuine crises and minor occurrences.

"Gauleiter. I am sorry to disturb you."

"It's too late for that. What is so important that couldn't wait until tomorrow morning?"

Zimmerman swallowed. "An urgent report, sir. Enemy bombers headed this way."

For a moment, Mutschmann wondered if the man was joking. "Toward Dresden, of all places?"

Zimmerman tensely nodded.

This has to be false information, Mutschmann thought. He decided to indulge his sergeant for a moment. "I see. And when is this attack supposed to happen?"

"Imminently, sir."

This was ludicrous, Mutschmann thought. *Just another in what seemed to an endless number of false alarms based on fantasy and fear.* "And the purpose of this supposed strike would be...."

Zimmerman was stuck for an answer. "I have no idea, sir. I'm merely—"

Mutschmann, completely exasperated, sneered, "You waste my time with rumors and are befuddled by the simplest questions? Why would the Allies possibly strike Dresden? Have they grown tired of bombing Berlin? Perhaps they think destroying the Opera House, the public gardens will break our will?"

"There is the munitions manufacturing, other—"

"Don't be ridiculous. Whoever issued this message is incompetent, and you should know that."

Zimmerman flushed in embarrassment. "I'm just doing my duty, sir, as you have repeatedly advised me to do it. I'm sorry I made you angry."

Mutschmann took a step closer. *Apparently, this fool was like some of his guests,* he thought, *believing that the end was very near. Hogwash.*

Mutschmann leaned closer still, making no effort to conceal his anger. He hissed, "So you have no faith in the Party, in the Führer, in me! There is a place on the Eastern front for doubters like you. Leave my home immediately! I'll deal with you tomorrow. Heil Hitler!"

Pulse pounding, Mutschmann angrily turned and headed back to rejoin the party. Inge, holding a half empty wine glass in her hand, greeted him cheerily as he returned to the main room. Regaining his composure, he smiled back, looked at her striking features, including her handsome face, and said, "You should really plan to visit my command center in the next few days. You will be most welcome, indeed."

GISELA, ALBERT, AND THEIR FAMILIES
February 13, 1945
The First Wave Strikes

TIME WAS RUNNING OUT FOR Gisela. Frantically, she rushed into the family apartment, startling her parents. The only way to bring her plan to fruition was to hope against hope that Matthias had finally come home. That little time was left, so he simply had to be at home.

He was not.

"You have to help me find him," she beseeched her parents.

"No," Gustav replied firmly. "Not until you tell us what is going on."

"All you need to know is that we must get him to the Dresden-Neustadt station by 21:00 hours."

Her parents still didn't understand, thinking she was referring to their forced deportation to take place early the next morning. Even though Gisela had no time to stand around, she confessed to them about Albert, showed them the pass, explained that it would be Matthias, not her, on the train. If Albert refused to cooperate, she would find another car for Matthias to ride on. He *would* be on the train.

"Please, help me find him. This is his only hope."

Hannah and Gustav finally understood Gisela's desperate pleas and knew that she was right. As dangerous as it was sending their beloved boy out of the city, perhaps completely on his own, this plan was a far better alternative than allowing him to leave Dresden, traveling on a train to far different destination.

For a moment, Gisela considered telling them about Gruber, but she realized it would only upset them. She looked at her own fate as sealed, either in the form of a local firing squad or being butchered in some awful way in the Stutthof death camp.

"I saw some children playing near the Frauenkirche. Perhaps he's joined that group over there. I'll go in that direction. We must find him and save him!" Her parents nodded in agreement.

No sooner had the words left Gisela's mouth than they heard an eerie, chilling sound echoing in the distance. The mournful wail of air raid sirens.

Hannah was distraught. "Oh, no! Another of these awful drills." Then she brightened. "The sirens might cause Matthias to return home quickly."

Although Gisela was equally familiar with the endless series of false alarms over the past months, she was on full alert. Something told her this was no drill. Whatever the case, they had to find Matthias and get him out of Dresden.

Grabbing their coats and moving toward the front door, the next sound that Gisela and her parents heard froze them where they stood. It was not sirens nor the thunder of the still-distant Lancasters, but the persistent buzz of the wave of De Havilland Mosquitos, off in the distance and flying well in advance of the heavy bombers. The Mosquitos were unique in that their frames were primarily constructed of wood, allowing them to fly light, fast, and agile at speeds more than 100 miles faster than the cumbersome Lancasters. Nine of them would soon be maneuvering into position to mark the main bombing locations.

As Gisela, Gustav, and Hannah ran into the street, they looked up to see the inky winter sky beginning to sparkle with what looked like a shower of bright, green and white falling stars, elegantly cascading toward earth—magnesium parachute flares spilling out of the bellies of the Mosquitoes by the thousands.

The Germans had come to call these marking flares "Christmas trees." Their purpose was not to delight or awe, but to illuminate targets at night so that the bombers could more accurately obliterate their targets. The city now started to glow in the silvery-white light, bright as day.

Gustav knew precisely what they were. "My God. They are going to bomb us!"

At the same moment, the Schmidts were sitting with hundreds of other people in the brightly colored, round-top tent on the banks of the Elbe. The Circus Sarrasini was a permanent fixture in town. A team of colorfully decorated acrobatic equestrians had Rudy and Karl dazzled as they performed tricks on the backs of powerful Arabian horses. They did handstands, somersaults, even pulled themselves under the galloping animals' bellies and back up into the saddle on the opposite side.

The crowd clapped and shouted its approval as the ebullient music of a calliope filled the tent—all but drowning out the cry of the air raid sirens and the growing hum of the Mosquitos. Rudy saw the bright sky filtering through the tent's canvas roof. He assumed it was part of the show, but Mr. Schmidt, also looking up, knew better.

Meanwhile, Albert was standing with hundreds of others around the train station and the platform. The cascading lights appearing above them had an entrancing effect. A young mother, on a bench nursing her thin and frail baby, looked up, beaming, the dazzling display of falling sparklers a sharp contrast to the dull gray that her world had become.

Around her, people of all ages, some of them roused from sleep, focused their eyes on the sky, not understanding what was happening. Albert deduced that blaring sirens accompanied by descending flares portended a bombing attack—how serious he had no idea. What was he to do? Seek some sort of shelter or wait until the last possible moment for Gisela to arrive? He saw a clock on a tower. Fortunately, the train had not yet arrived at the station—it was running a little late.

He couldn't conceive why the enemy would bomb Dresden. Like so many others, he believed the innocent cultural city myth. Facing reality, he understood that once the bombing started, no doubt in a terrifyingly short amount of time, the train station, the trains, and hundreds of refugees not able to get in the shelter under the building, would be obliterated.

The glare from the "Christmas trees" was now so bright that he had to shield his eyes. His goal of meeting and escaping with Gisela was becoming hopeless.

"Run!" he yelled at the top of his lungs. "Find shelter!" As those nearby looked at him uncomprehendingly and the flares traced their inexorable path downward, Albert realized there was no place for him to hide as he shoved his way through the crowd.

As a beautiful girl in a leotard vaulted off the back of a massive, chestnut Hanoverian steed, Mrs. Schmidt felt a stirring in her belly. She had noticed the contractions growing in frequency and intensity for the past half-hour. Having been through childbirth before, she now worried that her water would break at any moment. She nudged her husband and spoke softly in his ear, telling him it was time to go to the hospital, not noticing the concerned ringmaster talking animatedly with an air warden next to the grandstand.

The ringmaster, face turning pale, strode to the musicians positioned next to the main ring of the circus and motioned for them to stop playing. As the music died, a murmur of confusion and concern swept through the tent. Others saw that the night sky was ablaze with light. The ringmaster grabbed an overhead microphone and ran into the middle of the ring, gamely trying to maintain a sunny disposition.

"Forgive me ladies and gentlemen, but it appears that a situation is developing. At this time I would ask that you leave your seats and head outside in an orderly fashion." The murmur that had circulated through the crowd transformed into the sharp edge of panic.

Mrs. Schmidt looked with grave concern to her husband. "What's happening?" He was ashen, and she realized that survival was their overriding challenge. Somehow they had to get out ahead of everyone else, make their way to the family car. Fortunately, the hospital was only a matter of blocks away. Surely they would be safe there, and her baby could be born without incident.

"I can assure you, there is no cause for alarm," said the ringmaster, fearing a mad rush for the exits as the buzzing sound of the Mosquitos filled the tent. Schmidt knew that they only had moments to find shelter. He gathered his family and pressed them into the surge toward the openings in the tent's flaps. Amazingly, the twins cooperated out of obvious fear for their lives.

Mutschmann and his guests were drinking and laughing during a giddy round of charades, fueled by flutes of Moët & Chandon that never seemed to empty. Over a cascade of raucous laughter, a stout woman dressed as Marie Antoinette screamed for everyone to be quiet. As the chatter stopped, for the first time they clearly heard the echo of the air-raid sirens, loud and insistent.

Very drunken Inge snuggled up to Mutschmann and whispered: "Promise to save me." He responded softly with a worried smile, "Don't be scared, my dear," even though he now had knowledge that a massive bombing raid was about to strike Dresden.

The descending Christmas trees, now close enough to the ground to illuminate the streets brighter than daylight, also mesmerized Matthias and his friends as they did so many others looking upward. It was all too exciting. "Fireworks!" said Matthias breathlessly to his exhausted friends.

Albert tried to push his way through the crowd, but it was impossible—full-blown panic had set in and he was part of a tangle of bodies shoving and jostling, headed anyplace but there. Albert's first awareness of the approaching wave of Lancasters was the deep rumble emanating from a distance, still hidden in the darkness of the sky. He squinted and thought he could make out dark shapes moving closer to the city's skyline, the sound of engines like an approaching tornado.

Desperately scouring the crowd for any sign of Gisela, he suspected it was already too late, even if he saw her, the bombs would strike before he could reach her—or she could reach him.

"Attention!" came the cold, metallic voice through the bull-horns positioned along the platform. "Major enemy forces are now approaching the city area. Bombing is expected. Seek cover immediately. Do your best to get underground…."

Albert was already in motion. Using his good arm, he wrestled his way through the masses, even as he tried to block out the shouts and cries and screams of terror. Shoving aside a handcart, he finally made it to the street running adjacent to the platform and raced in the direction of the Jewish ghetto.

Mutschmann, with Inge clinging tightly to him, followed his guests to the windows to see what all the excitement was about. Zimmerman's warning was echoing loudly in his ears, but the report couldn't possibly be true. Bombing Dresden made no sense. The city was a seat of culture, centuries-old architecture, gardens, and palaces.

When he saw the sky speckled with bright flares, the wave of Lancasters relentlessly making their way over the horizon, Mutschmann would forgive Zimmerman, not discipline him if tomorrow still existed. This unexpected attack remained inconceivable to him. "Everyone, to my shelter. The raid will be over quickly." His flustered wife Minna led the panicked guests underground.

Napoleon looked at Mutschmann aghast. Totally confused, he demanded: "How can it possibly be over quickly? We have no antiaircraft guns. You allowed the SS to move our defensive weapons to the Eastern front for use in driving back the Red army. We're helpless!"

Mutschmann dismissed him with a slight, contemptuous smirk. "Bring along the champagne," he shouted.

These words did not appeal to clingy Inge, now feeling so hopelessly drunk that she backed off from the Gauleiter rather than throw up on him. Almost falling over in racing toward the shelter, she bumped into her industrialist husband, twenty years her senior, and proceeded to heave on him. Fortunately, she did so before disappearing into the bunker where the acrid smell of her vomit would have caused much discomfort among Dresden's Aryan elite.

At almost the precise moment that Inge retched, the bomb doors of the first wave of Lancasters opened, and dotted lines of streaming bombs began falling.

Gustav, meanwhile, was the first to hear the whistling of the bombs. He screamed over the din, "We must get back to our cellar!"

Gisela looked at him in utter distress. "But Matthias—"

"There is no time left. We can't help him if we're dead!"

Pandemonium ruled at the Circus Sarrasini. Fraught with terror, people raced for any semblance of cover they could find, dragging their children with them, taking no notice of those who had fallen or were frantically begging for help. That was when the first bombs and incendiaries hit.

Massive percussions rocked the ground—so powerful that they toppled buildings, raining bricks and timber and twisted metal onto the life-threatened, fleeing crowd. Incendiaries ignited wooden roofs, sparking lesser explosions as fuel tanks erupted in flames. The clear night was now a gray-orange haze of smoke, spreading fire, and blinding dust.

Many collapsed where they stood. Thousands of others felt their bones shatter, their lungs collapse, as the shock waves hurtled them through the air, slammed them against buildings, even as they felt the very earth disappear below them. Others were buried alive in heaps of falling debris.

For those still standing, still hoping to find some refuge of preservation, they struggled to get their bearings, to decide in what direction they should attempt to flee. Blockbuster bombs blew up whole buildings, even as consuming fires spread everywhere while sucking all the oxygen out of the air. A massive firestorm, with winds comparable to those in a tornado, was in the making. A cascade of thunder, blazing heat, and death was now spreading from street to street to street throughout the central city. Dresden was ablaze.

The Schmidts were able to reach their family car, even as Mrs. Schmidt's water broke. Mr. Schmidt, with laser focus, would try to get to the hospital. Once in the vehicle, hoping for good luck while praying to God, he drove through the maelstrom of falling buildings and people scrambling for their lives.

Rudy and Karl huddled in tiny balls on the floorboard of the rear seats, covered by blankets. Mrs. Schmidt, sweating heavily, her face etched in pain, drew upon every bit of strength and courage she had, trying to breathe through the increasingly sharp contractions, mumbling to herself that her baby had to live.

Mr. Schmidt was no longer sure of the correct direction to the Carolahaus Hospital. Through the dense smoke he couldn't read street signs, the bombs having knocked heavy debris into the streets, making them nearly impassable.

He arbitrarily jerked the wheel to the left onto another street just as the block behind them exploded, billowing out dark clouds of pulverized stone and dust. Mrs. Schmidt saw a man, now a human torch, running alongside the car in agony, phosphorus from the first incendiaries clinging to him like jelly. Another cluster of incendiary bombs ignited before them, momentarily blinding Mr. Schmidt. Mrs. Schmidt doubled over, instinctively shielding her unborn baby from the blast of heat that felt as if it would scorch them alive.

Gisela, her parents, and other neighbors who had managed to make their way into the building's cellar, huddled in the Stygian darkness, as the earth rocked and shook, thunderous blasts knocking loose huge piece of concrete from the building's foundation, rupturing gas lines, pummeling them with rocks and dirt. Many of them shared the same terrifying thought: This could be what their lives led to, being buried alive.

Gisela would harbor no such fear. She had come too far, fought too hard to concede anything to death just yet. She drew her knees further into her chest as she curled up on the shaking floor, closed her eyes, and concentrated on regulating her breath. The noise and power of the bombs was nearly incomprehensible.

"Plug your ears!" Gustav bellowed into the darkness. "Put your fists in your mouth so your ear drums don't rupture!"

Miraculously, through the smoke and the fire and the dead and dying, Mr. Schmidt could now see the vaguest outline of the Carolahaus Hospital. Equally miraculously, the building was still standing. He drove as quickly as he could beneath the searing, yellow-orange clouds hanging over the Altstadt area like a fiery pall. He struggled to keep the car moving forward, despite the incessant concussions that threatened to wrest the steering wheel from his hands and the blinding white-hot flashes caused by the incendiaries and spreading fires.

Above, the Lancasters continued to roll in, wave after wave. Schmidt braked hard to avoid hitting a family huddled over a man whose head was bleeding from a gaping wound. The car was now just steps from the hospital's entrance. "Get out!" he shouted to the others, as he angled the car in the middle of the rubble-strewn street. He threw open his door, raced to the passenger side to help his wife exit the vehicle, while also pulling Rudy and Karl close. Assaulted by embers and falling pieces of building material, they made their way through the choking fog and fire into the hospital entrance.

At almost the same time, Heinz, tears streaming down his face, stood over the body of his friend dressed like a red devil, now prone on the rocking pavement, his skull crushed by a jagged chunk of concrete. As their world came crumbling down on them, Matthias instinctively realized that they had to find cover. He saw the arched doorway of a building that was still intact. He grabbed Heinz by the arm and pulled him in that direction.

For Gisela and the others in the cellar, it seemed as if the thundering would never end. How could there possibly be these many bombs? How many planes could there be? She opened her eyes long enough to see her family and neighbors, covered in dirt and ash and rubble, crying and shaking. She hoped that those who were motionless were still breathing. She could hear Weinblatt praying. "Shield and shelter us beneath the shadow of Your wings. Defend us against enemies, illness, war, famine, and sorrow...."

Then, as quickly as the bombarding had started, it began to taper off. Within the span of a minute, the explosions had rumbled to a virtual stop. The actual bombing run lasted for less than twenty minutes, even though those on the ground thought that an hour or more had passed.

Gisela opened her eyes again. The cellar was a jumble of dislodged beams, twisted rebar, and gouged hunks of concrete. Her mouth filled with dust, her eyes burning. Gisela surveyed the wreckage, illuminated by shafts of light that pierced the darkness from the fires above, penetrating the cracks in the cellar's foundation.

Many of those who had been motionless remained so, some of their bodies so badly twisted and shattered that there could be no hope of their being alive. With a burst of relief, Gisela saw that her parents were badly shaken, but still breathing. The others were in varying states of shock, many crying out in pain from their broken bones or bleeding heads and torsos. Fearing that the peaceful lull was to be short-lived, no one dared speak. Eventually, Weinblatt broke the silence. "Do you think it is safe to go up?"

Gisela pulled herself to her feet, using pieces of crumpled building as leverage. She was cut and bruised, but nothing seemed to be broken. "Wait here." Seeing that the stairway leading out of the cellar was still somewhat intact, she picked her way through the rubble and began making her way up toward the street.

No one could have been prepared for the sight. Stepping outside, the fires accosted every sense in her body, almost taking her breath away. The entire block, what was still there anyway, seemed to be engulfed in searing flames that felt as though they might melt Gisela's skin.

Small bands of dazed survivors who had also dared to venture out moved aimlessly between giant mounds of rubble, ducking scorching tongues of fire that erupted without warning from gaps in crumbled walls, even from fissures in the earth itself.

Gisela saw the blackened arms and hands of her neighbors trying to claw their way out of shattered buildings while avoiding heaps of smoldering debris. Enormous craters dotted the street and sidewalks, and massive stores of burning lumber, bricks, twisted metal glowing red, and fallen stones made traversing from block to block virtually impossible.

Just ahead, a lump of gray ash moved, and Gisela realized it was a human being. She stumbled toward the middle-aged woman. Gisela didn't recognize her. The woman peered up at Gisela as if looking at an apparition. She mumbled something unintelligible and weakly reached for Gisela, clutching at the air with gray, bloodied fingers.

Gisela started to offer words of encouragement, but the woman's body shuddered, and her arm fell lifelessly to the ground.

With chunks of burning debris falling everywhere, Gisela realized that she could be crushed at any moment. But the rubble and fire didn't impede her focus and unflagging determination.

"Matthias!" she cried out. "Matthias!"

Gisela ran past burning buildings; the heat was almost overpowering. She took her shawl and wrapped it around her head and face. She felt some small measure of relief in dealing with the choking smoke being belched out by so many ubiquitous fires.

Albert, meanwhile, stumbled toward where he guessed Pulnitzerstrasse might be, bloodied and dazed. He had not found much shelter but had simply fallen to the cobblestones and pulled himself into a fetal position as the bombs fell. His ears rang, his face was caked in ash and dust, but miraculously, while so many buildings fell and burned around him, he had survived. The train station was a smoldering rubble. His only thought now was to find Gisela, hopefully still alive.

Bursting fires surrounded him; the streets littered with charred bodies. He coughed and rubbed his eyes. *This smoke will kill me.* He reached into his knapsack, found a scarf and placed it over his nose and mouth. He pressed on as if in a horrible dream. There were cars aflame, and the bodies of men, women, and children—soldiers, refugees, civilians—scattered about. Wherever he looked, he saw pandemonium, chaos, and human destruction.

He tried to get his bearings, but the streets were a disorienting maze. Everywhere, people continued to stream out of broken buildings only to look around as if somehow they had been transported to the surface of some alien planet.

Mrs. Schmidt lay on a table, ringed by candles in what just a little more than an hour earlier was an administrative office. The wing of the hospital that housed surgical rooms had been reduced to dust.

"Push," said a nun, calmly but firmly. "The baby's head is crowning. Push!" Mr. Schmidt, Karl, and Rudy sat, stunned, in a nearby hallway as burned, wounded, and broken people flooded in. The handful of hospital personnel who were not injured or dead themselves did the best they could to offer assistance, but they were simply overwhelmed. Nearby a man tried to explain to a woman cradling her dying child that he was a janitor, not a doctor.

"Matthias!" Gisela's voice was swallowed up by the inferno. She'd found that if she walked in the middle of the street, she stood a better chance of avoiding being crushed or ignited.

As she rounded a corner, she came upon a distraught woman standing outside a building fully engulfed in flames. She looked at Gisela, eyes filled with utter desperation.

"My babies. They're inside. Please!" Gisela turned toward what was left of the structure. No one inside could possibly still be alive. The woman could read Gisela's reaction. "No," she said quietly. Then, in a scream, "No!" She charged toward the building's entrance.

Gisela tried to stop her, but the woman disappeared inside just as the fractured wooden eaves gave way and the structure collapsed in on itself with a ghastly thud, spraying rubble and blasting hot air at Gisela, who crashed to the ground, covering herself.

Once the wave of heat had subsided, she clambered to her feet. Which direction to go? Every choice seemed equally impossible, cloaked in death and destruction. As she had countless times before, Gisela reached deep into her inner strength and somehow found the motivation to press on. "Matthias!"

As she wandered from street to street, observing air-raid wardens, fire crews, and volunteers of all kinds trying to bring thousands of fires under control, she lost track of time. Where was Matthias? Was he still alive? Was he dead? Or had he by some miracle escaped?

Continuing her search, Gisela found a safe location to sit down and rest—just for a few minutes. *I need to stop for a moment or two*, she said to herself, *then I'll continue my search.* She dozed off, dreaming of chaos all around her. Waking up in a foggy haze, she could not believe that she had slept for as long as she had—longer than an hour, closer to two hours.

Gisela struggled to her feet, tried to clean off the dust caked on her body, and started walking, now unsure where she was or what she was doing. Gathering together her wits, she remembered and again screamed out, "Matthias! Matthias!"

She thought she heard a low, rumbling sound, somewhere off in the distance. It was not what she wanted to hear, Matthias's voice— but rather a deep, rumbling sound emanating from the northwest. In disbelief, Gisela whirled and fixed her gaze on the horizon. For a moment, she wasn't sure whether to run or remain stationary. Lancaster bombers, once again, were beginning to darken the sky.

The second wave of the planned assault on Dresden was about to release another deadly round of hell fire and fury.

WALLACE
February 13, 1945
Four hours before the Second Wave Attack

LINE AFTER LINE OF FOUR-ENGINE Lancaster heavy bombers sat quietly on the runway as twilight eased into evening darkness. RAF crews in flight gear streamed toward these craft, carrying flasks of hot tea and sandwiches. As they did so, they had learned to push aside their fears. From their demeanor, they could well have been laborers heading to lorries that would ferry them to a construction site.

Wallace, ever meticulous, carefully inspected *Thumper*, a sturdy if slightly scarred bomber with a caricature of the Disney cartoon rabbit creatively painted on each side near the plane's nose. He looked for low tires and bent wings or gear struts while also making sure the tail assembly was in fully operational condition.

Then he approached a lead mechanic. "You stripped off the extra armor?" Wallace queried, just to make sure he understood.

"No choice, mate. You've got a one-thousand kilometer flight each way with seven tons of payload!" The mechanic eyed the bomber with pride. "Twice what the Yank Flying Fortress, the B-17, can muster."

Wallace greeted this insight with something less than pride. *Just means more bombs to wipe out more innocent lives*, he thought to himself.

"Ready to fly?" came a voice from behind him. Wallace turned around to see Chaplain Hendricks coming toward him, flanked by members of the bomber's crew. Tail gunner Tom O'Malley gave Wallace a big smile. "Here we go again," he said airily.

Walking with O'Malley and Hendricks was navigator Harry Murray, radio operator Liam Smithson, and bombardier Charlie "Dead Eye" Maxson. Each of them admired their captain, viewed him as a hero, especially for piloting them home alive from their last mission to Berlin.

Hanging back slightly were two young men, including an Aussie named Bert Anderson, who was replacing upper turret gunner Freddie Richmond. With him was Frank Sanderson, having received orders to replace Oliver Brannan. Bert, who had not yet turned twenty, was about to embark on his first flight. Wallace could detect a little fear in his eyes, but Frank, at twenty-four, had flown around ten missions as a flight engineer before his Lancaster landed awkwardly and caught on fire. *Thumper* was to be his new ride.

Tail gunner Tom had an odd sense of humor. Trying to project confidence and swagger, he bellowed toward Hendricks, "Here to administer the last rights, eh, chaplain?"

Everyone grimaced. Wallace looked at him sternly, then said, "Tom, we need to pray for the souls of our two lost crew members. I'm grateful to Chaplain Hendricks for accepting my request to offer us a pre-flight prayer."

"Sorry, sir, I was out of place," Tom mumbled as his face turned bright red in embarrassment.

Hendricks spoke up. "Gentlemen, let's form a circle, link our hands together as brothers-in-arms, and bow our heads in prayer. Heavenly Father, I pray for our fallen friends who have given their all in the name of human freedom. May they rest forever in the palm of your loving hands. And, yes, we exhort you to watch over each and every crew member here this evening ready to carry out this critical bombing mission. Help them to function effectively as a team. Thank You for keeping Your all powerful arms around them, assuring them that nothing, not even death, can ever separate them from Your boundless love. So we humbly and gratefully thank You for all these blessings in the name of Your Son, our Savior Jesus Christ. Amen."

Off in the distance came the sound of a soft explosion. They all looked up and saw a green flare burst in the darkening sky, bathing Wallace, Hendricks, and the *Thumper*'s crew in a faint emerald hue.

Hendricks reached out and shook Wallace's hand. "God knows what's in your heart, my friend. As you've done so many times before, fly carefully and prayerfully through the valley of death and bring these men home safely."

Wallace regarded Hendricks grimly, thanking him. "I can only hope that this bombing run will convince these ruthless Nazi bastards finally to surrender and bring an end to the human slaughter of this endless war."

He then turned to his crew. "Everyone on board. Get ready for takeoff." Before boarding himself, he smiled at Hendricks and promised to bring the plane and crew safely back home—in one piece.

Within minutes, Wallace and Frank Sanderson had the four Rolls-Royce Merlin engines coughing, hesitating, then starting and humming. When *Thumper*'s turn came for takeoff, Wallace wheeled the plane toward the main runway. Once there and with engines at full throttle, *Thumper* raced down the main runway, picked up enough speed to have a smooth takeoff, and lifted into the air, ready to join the pathfinder group leading a long stream of more than 500 Lancasters eastward over Belgium to rain down more destruction on what was deeply bleeding Dresden.

Hendricks, meanwhile, stood by the command tower as ground crews moved swiftly among the bombers, knocking away the wheel chocks as the legion of propellers whirred into life, ready to punch through the cold nighttime air.

The chaplain knew that most crew members on every plane, as they went about their assigned duties, were repeating prayers to whatever higher power they believed in. He imagined them asking for divine blessings and for forgiveness of their sins, along with the hoped-for expectation of safely returning home to the Fulbeck Airfield where they could again feel the solid earth of their beloved England beneath their feet.

Before walking away from the airfield, Hendricks offered another silent prayer for each and every crew member on this mission, all of them courageous volunteers facing death every time they reached into the sky. And he took special note to commend Captain Wallace Campbell to the Lord's infinite love and care.

WALLACE
February 14, 1945
Second Wave Approaching Dresden

THUMPER HAD BEEN FLYING ABOVE a thick cloud cover, but coded messages from the first wave indicated that the sky over Dresden was clear. Off in the distance, some sixty miles from their target, Wallace could now see what looked like bright fires—a city in flames. Dresden was still brightly ablaze, even though nearly three hours had passed since the first wave of bombing.

With communications linkages destroyed, the people on the ground—desperately working to control the firestorm—had no idea this second stream was approaching them. They believed that they had survived when the first wave bombers flew away. They were wrong and were about to experience the full realities of total war.

The second wave bombers had also learned that no Luftwaffe aircraft, specifically the ever-dangerous Messerschmitt BF-110 night fighters, had appeared to challenge the first wave. The pickings were going to be easy, almost too easy, mused Wallace, with a renewed vision of needless killing beginning to dance around in his mind. He tried to ignore these thoughts, as if caught between a rock and a hard place, and he forced himself to paraphrase the advice given him by Colonel Burton and Chaplain Hendricks:

"No one relishes hitting unprotected targets with high civilian populations. But if this brings this damn war to a quicker end, then there really is nothing else to consider at all."

Wallace spoke into his headset, asking navigator Harry Murray whether they had drifted slightly off course, no doubt caused by strong, high altitude winds.

Harry soon replied, his voice crackling into the intercom: "No problem. Just a degree off. Correction made. Right back on course."

"Oh, yes. More favorable news coming in," added radio operator Liam Smithson. "Still no cloud cover to hamper us. Just hope our pals in the first wave left us something to clean up. We can't miss this time."

Over his headset Wallace heard the chuckles from the other crew members. Suddenly, he felt an overwhelming urge to turn the bomber back to Fulbeck, payload intact, damn the consequences. But he knew the whole crew would challenge such insubordinate action. Still trying to control his brain, he concentrated on the oath he had taken upon joining the RAF: to be faithful and bear true allegiance to His Majesty King George VI, and do right by the people after the laws and usages of this realm....

Those who didn't believe in God had the option to conclude their oath by solemnly, sincerely and truly declaring and affirming their intentions. Yes, Wallace reminded himself, of course I believe, "so help me God." The same God, who as Hendricks had noted, hated evil. The God who had clearly commanded, "Thou shalt not kill."

Confusion was taking over Wallace's mind. He was the pilot, the one in command. Should he proceed toward the bright balls of fire, destruction, and death ahead, or should he pull out of the stream in defiance of his sworn military obligations? His mind turned to the loss of Anna and James. If he quit, would he be dishonoring them as well?

Seeking to steady his mind, he imagined the endless atrocities that Hitler and his Nazi fanatics had committed over the past several years—not only on his own family, but on all those vulnerable innocents who had suffered every human indignity simply because a few maniacs despised Jews or Gypsies or homosexuals or the enfeebled.

In all of his bombing runs going back more than three years, he now asked himself, hadn't he already punished innocent Germans enough for their unwillingness—perhaps lack of courage—to stand up to Hitler and his brutally authoritarian regime? Hadn't Hitler punished these same German people enough? Did those in Dresden deserve the horrible additional beating that the second wave was about to deliver? When and where do you stop the killing when the killing won't stop?

Wallace didn't know, but just ahead lay a crucial decision point for him. To ease his tortured mind, he offered up a quick prayer: "Dear God, I feel so lost. Please guide me and forgive me for what I'm about to do."

Seeking clarity, Wallace withdrew into a mental reverie, briefly losing any sense of time or place. He snapped out of it when the voice of navigator Harry Murray reported over the intercom, "Five minutes from target. Couldn't ask for better weather conditions. No flak. No resistance. Hang on! Here we go!"

As the *Thumper* began its descent to 12,000 feet, Wallace saw the dark skies of the countryside give way to spiraling plumes of white and purple. He and his flight engineer Frank Sanderson were cast in the bizarre, orange and red glow of what could have been a radiant sunset.

Bombardier Charlie Maxson, lying prone below Wallace, gazed at the approaching city below. "Sweet Jesus," he murmured into his headset.

Wallace could see the fires that must have covered several square miles. Even at this lower altitude where the temperatures are still normally cold, he could feel the heat rising from the burning city, what had been a lattice of streets and tree-lined boulevards now caught in an inferno of scorching flames.

"Won't be needing you to navigate us in on this one, Murray," Deadeye Charlie breathed into his headset.

Wallace's eyes remained fixed on the maelstrom appearing below.

"No," he announced over the intercom for all to hear, his jaw set. "We're not dropping our bombs. Charlie, As your captain, that's my decision."

Sanderson fixed him with a stare. "Captain. We have orders."

"Dear God, look for yourself, Frank. What's bloody left to bomb? What would be the damn point?!"

"Thirty seconds," Murray's voice crackled over the headsets.

Wallace was resolute. "Stand down, I said. We're going home."

Frank Sanderson vehemently shook his head. "Ignore that order," he spat into the intercom.

Wallace's eyes filled with cold fury. "Do not countermand me. You have no authority to do so."

Sanderson, the new man on board, responded, "If you won't complete the mission, make no mistake the rest of this crew and I will." Over the intercom navigator Murray butted into the conversation, "Come on, Frank, we all want to save your ass from the Glasshouse, or a hanging. You've saved us many times. Now we're going to save you. Fifteen seconds!"

"Let me add," said Sanderson calmly. "Don't jerk this plane out of line. Follow our orders, or I will relieve you of command, and we'll come back around and drop the bombs. If need be, I can fly this crate."

Wallace refused to respond. His hands locked on the steering mechanism, he had to decide. He said to himself: *I'll be court-martialed; so what? My name—Anna, James…their lives taken…why?*

"Ten seconds. Nine, eight…."

Wallace held the plane steady. The burning city below was now a mute testament to the nauseating reality that power-hungry dictators could and would, if unchecked, destroy civilization itself. One bomber's payload would not really matter one way or another when the world had lost control of itself and human butchery had not yet found the means to restrain itself.

Inside his mind, Wallace grimaced. He had to accept that his personal feelings had to submit to wartime realities. If he was truly conflicted about the Dresden mission, he never should have gotten into this airplane in the first place. Burton had given him that option, but he made the decision to execute his duty. He had cast his die and should not have allowed himself to get tangled up again in personal feelings and second-guessing himself.

"Release the bombs," Wallace said into his headset.

At his utterance, the bombardier hit the switches before him. *Thumper* now completed its assignment, what the whole crew had committed to.

"Bombs away!" announced Deadeye Maxson.

Wallace didn't have to look down to know what was taking place. A barrage of bombs from *Thumper* and the other planes were now screaming toward the ground. For the next several seconds all would be quiet, except the whirring sound of the descending incendiaries and blockbusters, and then....

GISELA, ALBERT, AND THEIR FAMILIES
The Second Wave Strikes

G USTAV AND HANNAH COULD SEE and hear the new stream of Lancasters starting to drone overhead. They hoped that this would be a small wave, since so little inside the city limits seemed left to destroy. Like thousands of others, Gisela's parents busied themselves sifting through the debris, urgently looking both for possible survivors and prized personal possessions. From beneath a pile of concrete and wood, they could hear muffled groans. How many, it was impossible to know. How deeply were they buried—only trying to dig them out would provide the answer?

Hannah cast another fearful glance upward to see the oncoming Lancasters.

"Don't worry, my love," said Gustav. "They can only be assessing the damage. The worst of the bombing has to be over."

The next sound they heard was the awful whirring of a fresh fusillade of bombs as they spilled out of the Lancasters and plummeted toward them. For a moment, Gustav couldn't conceive that what he was hearing was real.

Gustav grabbed Hannah by her arm, and they scrambled back toward the small opening that led to the cellar. All along the block, all across the city, those who could still move scurried below ground for cover. A young boy, no older than Matthias, paused to look up. He wondered how the sky above him could possibly hold so many aircraft.

Less than a mile away from what he believed to be Pulnitzerstrasse, Albert also stood, helplessly transfixed by the terrifying spectacle. As he heard a cacophony of screaming bombs hurtling downward, he looked frantically about to see groups of people running aimlessly, looking for somewhere—anywhere—to hide, completely exposed. Albert knew they all had but one chance.

"The river! Run!" he said, animatedly gesturing in the direction of the Elbe. He took off running, still screaming and pointing, and many of the others followed after him as the next torrent of bombs and incendiaries hit the ground, shaking the earth to its core.

Gustav and Hannah finally managed to stumble down the broken stairs into the cellar as the thunderous percussions rocked the world above. Crawling their way into a corner, Gustav pulled Hannah close as if his arms could somehow shield her.

"Our children!" she screamed.

He pulled her more tightly. "I'm sure they've found cover," he said, hoping his words didn't sound as forced and hollow to his wife as they did to him.

She looked at Gustav with a tear-stained face, a mask of fear and doubt.

He stroked her hair. "We will survive, Hannah. We will always—"

The next incendiary bomb felt as if it had slammed into the ground directly above them. The last thing Hannah saw was her husband's eyes as a metal furnace door, encased in a brick wall, blew off its hinges and hurtled across the cellar like a cannonball—slamming directly into Gustav and Hannah as they clung to one another. Then, for them, all was dark.

As for Mutschmann and his guests, they had also ventured outside his bomb shelter after the first wave had subsided. Like most everyone in Dresden, they had believed the initial assault represented the extent of the Allied attack. How could it not be? They stood in disbelief as they watched Dresden burn.

Minna, along with the Gauleiter himself, invited their guests to stay on for the night. None of them could be sure that they would be able to get to their homes through the fires and ruins—assuming that their homes still existed.

Napoleon said thank you but no thank you. Furious about what he had witnessed, he wanted no more of Mutschmann, whom he held responsible for allowing the city to become defenseless. "It's your fault, sir," he told the Gauleiter as he left with his wife in tow. "We are going to lose this war!"

Other guests were more dazed and tired than angry. The hour had moved past midnight, and, as a group bloated on rich food and alcohol, they had no idea what to do or where else to go. They seemed totally disoriented.

Inge, having long since recovered from her vomiting, had cleaned herself and her husband up. She was once again on the prowl for Mutschmann. "Oh, come on my powerful leader," she winked at him, "you can wave your magic wand and clean up the city in a day or two. I know a strong man like you can do that." The Gauleiter just grimaced, moved across the room, and hung as close as he could to Minna.

Scared and sleepy guests started reviving when the deafening drone of the second wave was coming over the horizon. As the fresh onslaught of bombs and incendiaries began raining down, they desperately ran to the beckoning entrance to Mutschmann's bunker, the only one of its kind in the city.

Mutschmann had nearly made it to safety when he heard the shrieking whistle of a bomb descending directly toward his neighborhood. Overcome with fury and abject disbelief that another attack was happening, he ripped his Luger from his belt and began firing up into the night sky, as if he could destroy the Lancasters.

An incendiary bomb touched down within an eighth of a mile where he stood, detonating and swallowing up a few of his party-goers in a white-gold orb. The blast stunned and knocked Mutschmann down, but he slowly regained his senses and scrambled into the bunker.

As Albert reached the banks of the blackened Elbe River, he gave a final look back. What exactly he was looking for, he couldn't be sure—perhaps he imagined that Gisela would be there, running toward him and that he could rescue her.

He would take her by the hand and lead her to the water and dip beneath the surface as the fire washed over them. They would emerge unscathed, and finally she might look at him as the way he remembered her looking at Jacob back in school. But Gisela was just his chimera. She was not there.

Instead, Albert saw the Lancasters pummeling away with their bombs, stoking the furnace that was once a city. As incendiary bombs burst, all but sucking the air out of his lungs. He watched as a giant cyclone formed, a fire devil, drawing the oxygen out of Dresden for over seven square miles. *Is that what it's like to die?* His lungs searing, his eyes feeling as if they would burn out in his head, he fell back into the river where everything was dark and cool and silent.

As Wallace banked *Thumper* and headed back toward Fulbeck, he and the others were met by a sight that defied their imagination. A red and orange cyclone churned above the city, reaching up for nearly three miles into the sky, carrying thousands of souls with it.

Wallace was numb. He turned his attention to the task at hand. Get these men home alive.

Gisela stumbled along, barely able to walk. Moments before she'd passed a fountain that was bone dry, now a chalice containing the mummified bodies to those who had sought sanctuary in its boiled waters. She tried to call out for her little brother, but nothing more than a dry croak would come out of her mouth.

Ahead, she saw a figure moving toward her, a white ghost silhouetted by the smoke and flames. As this seeming apparition drew closer, the ghost developed a form, discernible features, and Gisela found herself staring at Rachel.

As if compelled by an unseen force, the two friends raced for one another and embraced, clinging wildly to each other.

"They're all dead," Rachel finally managed. "All of them, I'm sure. Mother, father—"

Gisela held her hand, trying to offer some measure of comfort—not just for Rachel but also for herself. For all she knew, everyone she loved was dead as well. "We're alive, Rachel. You and me. And I need you to help me find Matthias. I need to keep looking for him. He still may be alive."

Rachel could do nothing but gape at the firestorm engulfing the city and then regard Gisela as if she was utterly and totally disconnected from reality.

"No," said Gisela stoutly. "He's alive. Stay here or go on if you wish, but I have to find him." She squeezed Rachel's hand and then picked a direction and headed that way.

Rachel, frozen, unable to feel or even think, watched her friend walk westward. Then, drawing on a reservoir of strength she hadn't known existed, followed after her.

THE THIRD WAVE
February 14, 1945
Just before Sunrise

AMERICAN COMMANDER U.S. AIR FORCES in Europe, General Carl "Tooey" Spaatz was to one day remember: "Without the B-17 bomber, we may have lost the war."

Widely known as the "Flying Fortress," the B-17 bomber lived up to the moniker, featuring a flight deck bristling with .50-caliber machine guns mounted in plexiglass bubbles that afforded the gunners a 360-degree view, capable of carrying a two-ton payload of bombs.

Renowned for its remarkable ability to remain air-worthy even after being pummeled by enemy fire, the B-17 featured a distinctive, large tail that gave it unmatched maneuverability for a plane of its size and an impressive stability during high-altitude bombing runs. One and a half million tons of bombs were dropped on Nazi Germany during the war, over a third of them delivered by B-17s.

Lead pilot David Shapiro tightened his grip on the throttle that jutted from a pedestal between him and his co-pilot Eddie Smith aboard the *Bountiful Betty*. A calm and steady presence, David possessed the qualities that made him an outstanding bomber pilot. He had an ability to stay focused and aware of potential danger, regardless of the situation. Self-discipline was his mantra. His comrades re-spected his skills—and good luck—in fighting off enemy aircraft.

David projected the toughness and resiliency born from being a Jewish boy growing up on the streets of Hoboken, where harass-ment from Italian and Irish gangs in his neighborhood was simply a way of life.

David had always retaliated against local bullies, even when his parents and his religion told him it was wrong. He remembered the guys on the corner, calling him and his friends "kikes" and "Hymies," giving them purposeful insults for supposedly killing Jesus. David found this ironic; if Jesus hadn't died, there'd be no Christians, right?

These, of course were thoughts he kept to himself, at least for as long as he could. He remembered the long talks he'd had with his father about wanting to stand up for himself, to beat the crap out of the bullies, to protect his Jewish heritage.

"We're held to a higher standard," his old man had told him. "Refusing to answer violence with violence isn't the same as laying down. God wants us to battle evil. Yet He wants us to do it on His terms. By standing strong. Violence always has to be the last resort."

David had tried to believe the way his dad did, but such reason-ing wasn't for him. He recalled the day some guys on the corner had gone after his buddy Maury, how he'd nearly punched some Italian punk into a coma. He could still see the look of disapproval his father had given him at dinner that night when he saw David's bruised and scraped knuckle and black eye.

David eventually understood that violence should always be the last resort. But sometimes striking back, hard and fast, was the only thing bullies understood. When it came to Jew-hating Nazis, David's father agreed. He also remembered his dad's look of approval when he told his parents of his enlistment in the Army Air Force to fight the biggest bully of them all—Adolf Hitler. Now, nearly four years later, David knew that the Allies had the Nazis on the ropes, and he was proud to be part of a major sortie he hoped would be delivering the final knockout punch.

David and the other pilots of the 1st Bombardment Division of the United States VIII Bomber Command had been told that Dresden, although a cultural center, was also an important industrial site for the Nazis and, therefore, was a justifiable bombing target. They'd been told that, as an adjunct to the British Operation. Their particular mission's objective was to ensure that factories, fuel storage supplies, and transportation hubs in and around Dresden would be completely obliterated.

Further, David had heard speculation that this overwhelming show of air power was to demonstrate to Stalin and his generals what America and Britain were capable of doing, should they pursue likely plans to expand the USSR's presence in Western Europe. Rumors were also circulating that USAAC 8th Air Force commander James Doolittle had vociferously opposed the bombing of Dresden, deeming it an unnecessary strike against a defenseless city with a large civilian and refugee population. David could only surmise that Spaatz had overruled Doolittle.

They were just 200 miles out from Dresden now, and David anticipated a safe, efficient bombing run for the more than 500 B-17s involved in this sortie. As always, David remained alert, taking nothing for granted. Yet he was as calm as he'd ever been on a mission, looking forward to finishing the job at Dresden, getting his crew members back home safely, and hastening the end of this goddam war. His longtime girlfriend Betty was waiting for him back in Hoboken, and he was greatly missing her.

He noted the rose tint on the horizon. Dawn was about to break.

GISELA
February 14, 1945
Just after Dawn

THE SUN CREPT OVER THE horizon, burning a dull orange through the ashy haze that was suffocating the city, still an inferno of uncontained, raging fires that would ultimately burn for over a week. Gisela and Rachel wandered amid the devastation, overcome by what happened, numb to the magnitude of their loss, powered only by the fading hope that somehow, amid the rubble, scorched bodies, and the groaning skeletons of the buildings, Matthias and others they loved were still alive. The pock-marked streets represented passageways between smoldering heaps of stone and metal.

The two of them walked past an empty baby carriage, next to which lay a mummified mother and infant. The carriage somehow was still intact. In the street ahead, a giant metallic bird lay awkwardly in the rubble, its right wing reaching up toward the amber sky, its talons clutching at nothing, its haughty beak now twisted and molten.

Gisela took a moment to realize that the bird was the *Reichsadler*, the Imperial Eagle that had adorned the front of Dresden's Gestapo headquarters in what had once been the city's famed Continental Hotel. Now this seat of power and terror had become…nothing, a void—the only indication that a building had ever stood on the blackened earth was the vague rectangular shape of what was its foundation.

Rachel approached the fallen eagle, also realizing what it meant. "Gone. All of it. The Gestapo. Our papers. Our records. The men who would take us. We are free...."

Gisela laughed at the ludicrousness of their discovery. They were the phoenix arising from the ashes. So arbitrary, so unfair. Life. Freedom. To do what? To go where?

She heard a heavy shuffling of feet, a primordial wail. She looked past Rachel to see a tiger, an elephant, and two plumed horses wandering through the wasteland. Her laughter suddenly turned to horror. The whole scene was all too surreal. In a world where anything was possible, suddenly nothing had meaning.

Then, beyond the escaped circus animals, through the acrid haze, she saw two small silhouettes trailing after the beasts as if in some sort of obscene, mocking parade. Two boys.

Matthias and Heinz.

Gisela caught the cry in her throat and raced toward them. If Matthias was surprised or happy to see that she was alive, that she had found him, he didn't show it. He merely stared at her uncomprehendingly, as if she was a character in his horrible dream. Only when he felt her arms embrace him could he accept the possibility that she was, in fact, real.

Rachel joined them and the four sobbed in an embrace. Gisela smoothed Matthias's hair and wiped away the tears that stained his ash-covered face in black rivulets. "What happened? Where did you go? I've looked everywhere for you."

"I just wanted to play with the others. Then we got lost."

Gisela turned her attention to Heinz, gently stroking his face as well. "It's all right. We're alive. It's over...."

Only then did she hear a distant rumble. Her first reaction was that the elephant had broken into a run and was coming toward them, but she quickly realized such a thought made no sense and that elephants don't sound like angry machines. She looked past the boys and saw the bombers coming over the horizon—the incoming wave of American B-17s.

"No," she shrieked. "Not possible!" She realized that when nothing had meaning, anything was possible.

"We've got to run," she said, taking Matthias and Heinz by their hands.

But Matthias remained rooted in place. "To where?"

Gisela's only thought was the river. Why, she didn't know, but in that moment water seemed like their only viable refuge.

Twelve thousand feet above, approaching what had been the Altstadt area, David kept his hands firmly on the controls, checking his bearings as the *Bountiful Betty* closed in on its assigned target. Through the haze, co-pilot Eddie ventured to look down at the city. But there was no central city left to bomb.

"David? Are you seeing this?"

By then David too was able to regard the flat, charred, ghostly specter of what had been one of Europe's grandest cities. He and Eddie glanced at each other.

"What the hell are we supposed to bomb?"

David looked to his left to see that several of the planes had opened their hatches, the dark lines of bombs starting to stream earthward. He then saw that many more were banking and heading for home without dropping their payloads.

As Gisela led the others into the bracing water, shepherding them through flotsam and bloated and floating bodies, the *Bountiful Betty* banked away, hatch doors firmly closed.

Gisela and the others grasped desperately for one another in the Elbe River as what little was left of Dresden was once again rocked by the fury of titans.

WALLACE
February 14, 1945
Early Morning

WEARILY, WALLACE HEADED FROM *THUMPER* back toward his barracks. Except for the relief and gratitude that the mission was behind him, he was otherwise numb.

He heard footsteps approaching him from behind and glanced back to see Frank Sanderson heading his way.

"Wallace!"

The last thing Wallace wanted was to engage in conversation. He couldn't imagine what Sanderson might have to say. Perhaps he wanted to tell Wallace that he was going to report his near-insubordination to their superiors. Maybe he would recommend that Wallace seek extended time off from future bombing runs. He didn't care. But, out of military respect, he stopped and turned to face his flight engineer.

"Listen, mate. What happened up there…. I was talking to the others." Sanderson felt winded, his face flushed from the exuberance of returning from the mission alive and the cold embrace of the pre-dawn wind. "As far as we're concerned, well, we don't think anyone else ever needs to know."

Wallace was surprised to feel a small burst of gratitude. Despite everything, he didn't want to emerge from this war with a blemish on his record and his name. "Thanks. I guess we did what we had to do."

"That we did, sir. Followed our orders. Completed our assignment."

Wallace nodded, and Sanderson gave him a hearty clap on the shoulder before heading off to rejoin their crewmates. Wallace watched him go, envying the good cheer that he and the others exuded at having another successful mission under their belts.

Continuing his walk to his barracks, Wallace saw a pilot in front of the officers' quarters, adjacent to the runway. In the pool of light cast by lamps along the front of the quarters, he watched this man lifting a baby as his two older children and wife embraced him.

He turned his gaze eastward to the horizon and saw the promising pink glow of dawn suffused through the dense ground fog. The world turns. Another day begins. Life goes on.

Wallace rubbed his face, then said in a soft prayer, "One day, Lord, I'm trusting you will help me understand."

AFTERMATH
March–April 1945

ALTHOUGH THE NAZIS KEPT MOUNTING ferocious, desperate defenses, they were running out of essential war goods and losing many square miles of territory. Still loyal to Hitler, hardened Nazi enthusiasts among them refused to accept the inevitability of complete defeat.

Even before the bombing of Dresden, the Red Army had butchered its way through most of Poland, getting in position to capture Berlin. Amazingly, Wehrmacht resistance kept the Soviets from officially taking what was left of Dresden until late April.

The Western Allies pushed eastward across the Rhine River, driving mostly dispirited and bedraggled German forces back, taking hundreds of thousands of prisoners of war in the process. The American 7th Army breached the German Siegfried Line and crossed the Rhine River into the heart of Germany in mid-March.

Desperate to provide basic supplies to their besieged forces, the Nazis forcefully requisitioned shoes, clothing, food, and weapons from their citizenry in a frantic effort known as the *Volksopfer*, or "sacrifice of the people." Trying to delay the Allies' advances, German forces sabotaged dikes and dams as they retreated, causing severe flooding and necessitating the use of amphibious vehicles by the British in order to transport troops and supplies.

British and American bombing sorties continued to pound German targets, including the Saxon City of Leipzig. Wallace reluctantly agreed to pilot *Thumper* in a February 23 attack on this city, which lay about seventy-five miles northwest of Dresden. He and his crew, facing no Luftwaffe opposition, returned safely to their Fulbeck base. This flight was his last as a Lancaster pilot. Wallace asked for ground duty, which filled his days with endless paperwork until he mustered out of the RAF later in 1945.

By April, the Allies had broken through German defenses in Italy. Soviet and American forces finally met that same month in Torgau, Germany, sixty miles south of Berlin. A week later, the Soviets marched into the German capital. On April 30, Adolf Hitler, who could not face the reality of seeing his perverted *Lebensraum* vision completely crushed, blew his own brains out underneath the Reich Chancellery building.

Beginning with Geli Raubal, Hitler's reign of human destruction from 1931 to 1945 had cost the lives of around 50 million people, plus the complete destruction of a nation he allegedly loved—so long as the people acquiesced to his every whim.

As the Allies continued their relentless advance, they entered dozens upon dozens of concentration camps filled with the sick, the starving, and the decomposing bodies of the dead. In almost every camp the Allies liberated, they discovered unburied corpses scattered carelessly around the grounds, and starving people locked in barracks without access to food or water.

Typhus eventually claimed the lives of many who had managed to evade the gas chambers. Some prisoners, although liberated, died from starvation, even after Allied soldiers were able to provide them with food; they were simply too emaciated and weak for their systems to adjust to the long denied bounty available to them.

Stutthof, where Gisela, Mathias, Hannah, Victor Weinblatt, and his wife, among other Dresden Jews, were to have been incarcerated, was among those merciless sites overwhelmed by the influx of thousands of prisoners that the Nazis imported from other such extermination camps. By May 1945, Stutthof's population had declined in numbers, but as many as 65,000 people, mostly Jews, had their lives snuffed out there. Russian forces liberated those few who had enough strength left in them to keep living.

SS Chief Heinrich Himmler, a person totally lacking in human empathy or basic integrity, saw an opportunity to save himself. Through intermediaries, he proposed to release a number of Jewish prisoners held at Stutthof in exchange for five million Swiss francs to be paid by Jewish organizations. Once deposited in a Swiss bank account, the money was to permit Jewish prisoners to enter Switzerland, where the Swedish Red Cross would ensure their transportation to Denmark.

Before he could realize his riches, Himmler swallowed a cyanide capsule that gave him a way out by instant death rather leaving this world as he had more than earned—a public hanging.

Accurate records about the fate of Gisela's fiancé Jacob, as with so many other Nazi victims, did not exist. What information there was had him transported to Buchenwald where he worked as a slave laborer until he collapsed from malnourishment and physical exhaustion. Most likely camp guards of the Gruber type shot him dead where he lay and then ordered other prisoners to throw his lifeless body into a common burial pit.

In Dresden, the devastation following the bombings was almost unspeakable. The number of persons buried in the rubble or consumed by flames could only be estimated. Eight weeks later, cleanup crews had counted over 20,000 corpses. Hundreds of people had climbed into a large water tank in the Altmarkt only to boil alive or drown.

For weeks, the remains of those mummified by the heat and firestorm could be seen piled in heaps, many so burned beyond recognition that no one could identify their remains. Many people, suffering from painful wounds or enduring the grief of losing their loved ones chose to end their pain by taking their own lives. Gisela's parents, like many of their neighbors, were among those forever gone. Miraculously, though, workers extracted from under the destroyed buildings hundreds of people who somehow survived.

The effort to assure survival began almost immediately after the attack had ended. Some 350,000 people were now homeless. Within three days, German officials were ready to hand out nearly 600,000 daily hot meals to those who had lost everything except their lives. Gauleiter Mutschmann instituted martial law, and those caught looting or spreading rumors about the inevitability of the Third Reich's fall faced summary executions.

Incredibly, Mutschmann had survived the second wave of bombing that had cost the lives of a few of his party guests. But his good fortune did not last long. When the Russians began to arrive in Dresden, Mutschmann attempted to escape, bringing along all his valuables—including his expensive carpets and collection of marionettes—with him. Instead, the Russians captured him and sent him under armed guard to Moscow. Authorities there repeatedly interrogated him and finally found the once mighty Gauleiter of Saxony guilty of war crimes. In 1947, having had enough of his obfuscating commentary, they put him to death by hanging.

As for Minna, no one seemed to take note of her whereabouts. She lived on until 1971, a forgotten Nazi hostess whose later years were anything but worth remembering. Partygoer Inge, on the other hand, became a favorite of the Moscow-trained communist leaders who replaced the likes of Mutschmann in Dresden and elsewhere in East Germany. Communist Party head Walter Ulbricht, who proved almost as adept as suppressing people's freedoms as Hitler, particularly enjoyed Inge's engaging personality whenever he visited postwar Dresden.

On an unseasonably warm day in April, a Soviet KV-2 heavy tank rumbled across a bridge that spanned the Elbe River, not far from the spot in where Gisela, Matthias, Rachel, and Heinz had sought refuge in the water the morning that more bombs came tumbling down from above. A patrol of thin, poorly supplied Soviet soldiers flanked the vehicle, weapons at the ready—SS snipers were a deadly reality. "You are in Soviet occupied territory, under the rule of Soviet law," a metallic voice blaring from a speaker affixed to the tank. "Surrender your weapons."

Residents of Dresden, old and young, unarmed and defeated, stood frozen as the Russians approached, viewing them with uncertainty and fear.

In front of what had once been a bank building, a middle-aged couple with tears in their eyes watched the Soviets coming toward them. The man pulled his wife close in an embrace, kissed her tenderly, and then produced a pistol. The bullet was not intended for the Russian soldiers. A shot rang out and as the woman crumpled to the pavement and the Soviets turned, rifles leveled, the man put the barrel of the gun into his mouth and squeezed the trigger a second time.

Just a block away, an old man hobbling down the cratered street on a self-constructed crutch, approached another Russian patrol, waving a white flag, smiling, with tears of relief. He called out a greeting to them in Russian that he had carefully memorized. A bony, hardened Soviet private regarded the old man for a moment and then, as if dealing with an exasperating pest, raised his rifle and shot him dead.

Several of his comrades chuckled as they continued on their way. Raping and killing indiscriminately would be among their contributions to the tragedy of Dresden.

Standing before the shattered skeleton of a building, a group of young Nazi soldiers, hands clasped behind their heads, stood facing the remains of a brick wall, a squad of Russian soldiers at their backs, carbines raised. A grave-looking sergeant assessed the Nazis, coolly and dispassionately. "Because you are Nazi fascists and enemies of the Soviet people, I can assure you that you will be treated in accordance with your crimes."

Rolf, the young Wehrmacht soldier who had sold the exit passes to Albert, stood with his nose pressed against the bricks, his body trembling, his eyes brimming with tears. Could he be so fortunate? Had the stories about Russian brutality been exaggerated? Would they show him mercy? After all, the war was almost over, and he was still very young. There was nothing to be gained from killing him. He presented no threat.

Those were Rolf's last thoughts as the brace of Russian carbines fired and he and his fellow Germans fell to the cobblestones, shot in their backs. The bullets that had found him had brought the merciful end he'd sought, killing him instantly, sparing him the pain of the subsequent volley that the Russians fired into the pile of bodies, ensuring that there would be no survivors.

A few weeks before that moment, Gisela, Rachel, Matthias and Heinz were making their way down a rutted dirt road in the German countryside. They had been following the northward course of the river, part of a long line of refugees and survivors that stretched over the horizon. Gisela was grateful that Matthias had refused her offer to carry him. Weary to the bone, she wasn't sure how she would have managed. Like the hundreds of despairing people around her, Gisela too was hungry, besides being distraught over the likely fate of her parents—but just grateful to be alive.

Months would pass before she learned about the death her father and mother, along with so many others with whom she had laughed and played and loved. Somehow, she had survived. Whatever the road ahead had to offer, she hoped for something much better than what she had left behind.

As they trudged toward a distant rail station where a train waited that they had been promised would take them farther westward, Gisela and the others passed by a group of Nazi POWs. They were resting and smoking cigarettes in the shade of a tree under the watchful eyes of American troops. Gisela scanned their faces, wondering if she might find Albert among them. She didn't recognize any of the weary, defeated faces that stared back at her.

Gisela thought that she would be comforted to see these detested Wehrmacht soldiers humbled, their uniforms disrespected, the swastika flag of the Nazi regime that they had so willingly—many unwillingly—served ripped asunder. But her heart was too weary to hate anymore, and she simply walked on.

Ahead, she heard the sputter of engines, accompanied by cheers. She squinted into the bright sun to observe a jeep bearing American GIs driving toward her. As the vehicle bounced down the road, the men handed out chocolate bars and packets of dehydrated milk to desperate, dirty, hungry hands.

Gisela fought her way through the swell of bodies that rose to greet the men, and grasping upward through the sea of arms, felt her fingers wrap around something solid. She could read enough English to understand the words "Hershey Chocolate." She felt her stomach tighten, her mouth water at the promise of food.

Instead, she peeled back the wrapper and handed it to Matthias. He took a bite and then, rather than wolfing it down, broke it into pieces and offered them to Gisela, Rachel, and Heinz. Overcome, she pulled him close, even as her tears of relief, thanks, and exhaustion spilled out.

Gisela paid no attention to a truck that rumbled past close behind the jeep, carrying former American prisoners and a few German civilians back from Dresden where they had participated in the seemingly endless task of cleaning up and restoring order. Had Albert cast his eyes down he might have seen the gaunt form of Gisela hugging Matthias, but he had chosen that moment to turn his face toward the warmth of the sun.

In the chaos following the bombing, Albert had thrown his uniform into the river and put on the clothes he had brought for the escape. As the city burned, he searched relentlessly for Gisela. He remained in Dresden as long as he could, continuing to look for her, asking if anyone had seen a woman that fit her description. No one offered him any hope. He learned that Gisela's parents, along with the Weinblatts, had not survived. He finally decided, for his own preservation, to end his search and leave Dresden before the advancing Soviet forces finally arrived.

After several days walking along a road, he'd met some American troops. His missing arm helped him sell his story, told in broken English, that he worked on a farm and that a thrasher accident had claimed his missing limb. Therefore, the German military deemed him unfit for service.

The Americans fed him and gave him shelter—and then told him he'd be part of the effort to clean up the city. He said he had spent time in Dresden, working diligently until the Russians were rumored to be near. He was sure they would kill him just because he was a young German male. The American GIs bought his tale and decided to protect him.

Had Albert known the object of his heartfelt concern and love was standing so near to him, he would have leaped from the truck, run to her and promised to stay by her side. As it were, he enjoyed the soothing feeling of the sun on his skin. By the time he opened his eyes to survey the line of refugees once again, they had moved on.

GISELA AND WALLACE
Fifty Years Later
Mid-May, 1995

THE REBUILDING OF THE *FRAUENKIRCHE* Cathedral did not happen easily. The bombing raid had severely damaged and caused the collapse of this centuries-old structure. In the post-war partition of Germany, Dresden found itself in the Soviet zone; and reconstructing a shrine to the Christian faith was not a priority for the mostly atheist communist East German government. Once rid of the communist regime after 1989 and reunited with Western Germany, the people of Dresden decided to restore the church as a visible symbol of their remarkable resilience.

The reunification of Germany resulted in a comprehensive fund-raising campaign. A team of historians, architects, and engineers set about the arduous task of sifting through what remained of the structure and identifying which pieces would be incorporated into the new structure.

The builders consulted plans that dated back to the eighteenth century, and they made every effort to reuse original materials. They studied old photographic images of the church, drew upon the memories of surviving worshippers, and paid consummate attention to every detail from the exact pigment of the original paint to the precise reconstruction of the cathedral's massive oak doors. The results were nothing short of extraordinary.

The *Frauenkirche* once again rose above the Dresden skyline, now capped by a new, magnificent golden orb and cross—provided by Britain—that spoke to the eternal hope for Godly blessed lives on planet Earth. The cross was largely made by a son of one of the British bomber crews who had helped destroy the original structure. The bronze statue of Martin Luther, the landmark severely damaged from the bombings, stood once again in front of *Frauenkirche*, an exact replica of the original work.

A man, now approaching eighty, looked around in awe at the cathedral's magnificent interior, awash in the golden glow of a thousand flames. Like the others in the packed sanctuary, he solemnly held a candle to honor those who had perished, all that had happened on that February night fifty years earlier. He cast his eyes over the faces of his fellow worshippers, noting a woman in her early seventies, her clear blue eyes studying the large cross and stained glass window above the altar. He saw the faces of others in the flickering light, many of them rejoicing through their tears. He felt his eyes moisten at the sight.

After the closing prayer, he stepped outside into the streets of Dresden and took in the rebuilt city with awe. For most of the young people busily living their lives, hurrying from here to there on important errands, this was the only Dresden they had ever known. A modern city, with older structures still being restored among the gleaming, new edifices, so many of which were the ugly but functional apartment buildings designed by the communists.

He heard a burst of laughter and glanced over to see a group of attractive, well-dressed people enjoying coffee at a street-corner café. He tried to imagine what that very spot would have looked like that night, even though he was visiting the city for the very first time in his life—from the ground. He thought about going back to his hotel, when he saw her again—the woman with the arresting eyes he had spotted in the cathedral. He noted that her blonde hair mixed colorfully with silver in the bright morning sun.

She walked the streets with the familiarity of someone who had grown up on them. Even though she was a stranger, for some reason he couldn't explain, he felt compelled to follow her.

He lingered as she crossed the street, then fell into pace several yards behind. She walked into the Grosser Garten. The magnificent flower beds were arrayed in color, carefully tended and nurtured in defiance of the winter chill. He saw her sit on a park bench and pull her jacket more closely around her as she watched a father and his teenage daughter gambol on a spacious lawn that had was assuming the rich green hues of springtime.

After a moment, the father pulled something from his pocket, and he grabbed his daughter's hand, leading her to the sparkling Carolasee pond where the girl laughed as they fed a hungry cluster of honking swans. The woman seemed to be enjoying herself almost as much as this father and daughter were.

Wallace made the decision and slowly approached her.

"Excuse me," he said in surprisingly good German, "may I speak with you?"

The woman turned her blue eyes on him, and he saw how they sparkled with life and dignity. "You are English? I could tell by your accent."

He smiled. "I am. For many years I've spent time learning your language."

Gisela studied his face and saw the gentleness and kindness. She motioned for Wallace to join her. For a moment, they shared the joy of watching the father and daughter at play.

"I used to come here with my father," Gisela finally offered. "So many years ago. We'd feed the swans. Afterwards, I'd eat pastry while he read the newspaper.

"Now it brings me great pleasure to watch my husband's little brother and my granddaughter enjoy the same kind of outings. Ernst was born the very night of the bombing and miraculously survived it all."

Wallace nodded. She might have been here that night. "I saw you in the church service. Were you in the city when—"

She kindly responded. "An apartment. Yes. Then the Jewish ghetto. So long ago. Another life. Another world."

Wallace's next words did not come easily. But he knew he had to confess them. Why else had he come?

"I piloted one of the Lancasters that bombed Dresden that night so long ago. Yes, I was one of them."

Gisela regarded him with a face free of accusation or rancor.

"I know there's no point," he said hesitantly, trying to stem the emotion. "None at all. But…. I'm sorry. I don't ask forgiveness. Only that…" He could hold back his tears no longer. He looked away, trying to regain his composure.

"Please," she said with a gentle hand to his shoulder. "There is no need for guilt."

He could barely stifle his emotions. "Too often I've felt that searing pain of guilt for over the past fifty years." He brought his eyes to meet hers, his soul laid bare.

Gisela left her hand where it lay. "So many died. But you must know—your bombs saved lives. My life." She thought of her father and mother. Weinblatt. All those she had loved. All that they had believed in. They had become part of her in a way that she never could have imagined. "Some might say it was the hand of God." Gisela was not sure why she said that, but she certainly felt that she had finally understood what God hath wrought, and why.

Wallace could muster no reply. Instead he simply looked past his new acquaintance and felt a purpose.

They sat together in silence before a man's voice gently intruded. "Gisela?"

Wallace turned to see what he assumed to be her husband standing behind them. He noted that the elderly man's left arm was missing from the shoulder down.

"Is everything all right?"

Gisela nodded softly before returning her attention to Wallace. "As for me and hundreds of other Jews, without fighting men like you, we would have all ended up dead."

From somewhere deep in the darkness, amid the pain and sorrow, Wallace felt a flicker of absolution course through him. "And was it worth it? All that happened…was it worth it?"

Again, Gisela nodded. "I can only hope so. What else is there, except hope—and even faith?"

She stood up, politely said goodbye, crossed to Albert and slipped her hand beneath his right arm. Wallace watched them walk away.

It was then that a group of children in costume darted by, startling a flock of colorful birds that fluttered into the air.

Wallace looked up as they flew across the sun, silhouetted by the bright, warm glow, but not blocking his view entirely. He smiled, thinking of his beloved Anna and James, and felt a long awaited peace in his soul.